QUEEN BEE

A DOMESTIC SUSPENSE THRILLER

HEATHER DAY GILBERT

Queen Bee

Cover Design by Elizabeth Mackey of Elizabeth Mackey Graphics

Subject: Thrillers / Psychological; Domestic Suspense

Author Information & Newsletter: http: / / www.
heatherdaygilbert.com

MORE BOOKS BY HEATHER DAY GILBERT:

Find Heather's books at https://heatherdaygilbert.com/my-novels/

CLEAN PSYCHOLOGICAL THRILLER:

Queen of Hearts

CLEAN COZY MYSTERY:

The 9-book *Barks & Beans Cafe* cozy mystery series

The 3-book *Exotic Pet-Sitter* cozy mystery series

CHRISTIAN MYSTERY/SUSPENSE:

A Murder in the Mountains 4-book mystery series

The *Hemlock Creek Suspense* 3-book series

VIKING HISTORICAL:

The *Vikings of the New World Saga* 2-book series

The *Tavland Vikings* 2-book series

The Distant Tide

Sign up for Heather's newsletter at https://heatherdaygilbert.com/ to receive a FREE ebook download of HOUSE BLEND, a standalone *Barks & Beans Cafe* mystery novella.

Find all Heather's books at her website here: **https://heatherdaygilbert.com/my-novels/**

QUEEN BEE:

There can only be one.

In an effort to shield her foster daughter from a stalker at school, Twila relocates to a farmstead in an Appalachian radio quiet zone. Alongside battered women who have taken shelter at Cooper's Corner, Twila and her mute teen hope to find sanctuary caring for cows, chickens, and honeybees.

But their peace turns out to be short-lived when a man with an injured ankle and a flimsy story shows up in the woods. Before Twila can shuttle him off to a doctor, a straight-line windstorm rips through the area, downing trees and power lines and cutting off the well water.

As tempers flare and dark sides surface, Twila realizes she can't trust anyone. When one of the women goes missing in the night, she fears the worst has happened.

Like a tenacious queen bee, Twila plans to sting first and ask questions later. If push comes to shove, she's ready to sacrifice herself so her traumatized daughter can finally live again.

FOREWORD

This book was finalized just before laws unexpectedly changed to allow for limited Wi-Fi in the National Radio Quiet Zone in Green Bank, West Virginia, which is the real-world setting of this story. Thank you for understanding why this fresh twist wasn't able to be incorporated into the storyline in time.

The derecho in this book is based on my family's personal experience with a ten-day power outage following the derecho of 2012, which wreaked incredible destruction throughout West Virginia.

I hope you'll enjoy this glimpse into my home state of wild and wonderful West Virginia.

-Heather

PROLOGUE

It's always handy when the insect steps directly into the spider's web.

Isabella Falzone has been a threat to me for far too long, even if she still can't remember what she saw the night her mother was shot. I've always known it's a matter of time until she did, and now she's started meeting with the school counselor. Even though she's mute, she might work through her traumatic experience and recall some detail that could destroy everything I've worked so hard to hide.

But now she's on the run, and she's running straight into my trap. If I can get her overprotective foster mom out of the way, just for a moment, I'll take my chances and eliminate the only person who witnessed what happened that night.

ONE

The undercarriage of my 2007 Honda rattled over the dusty potholes in the long, private driveway. "Here's hoping I'll have at least a little internet access, so I can connect with my clients," I said.

Izzy gave me a commiserative nod. She was fifteen, and our temporary move into a radio quiet zone would probably affect her even more than it did me. But I had no choice, since a man had started stalking Izzy outside her private school. The police hadn't been able to track him down, and, even though the school tried to protect her, they couldn't guarantee they'd have eyes on her at all times.

Izzy's CPS case worker had told me about Cooper's Corner, a working farm that doubled as a women's shelter. It was nestled up against a mountain near the Green Bank Observatory in West Virginia. The farm was about as off-grid as it got, since cell phone, Wi-Fi, and Bluetooth were restricted in the radio quiet zone. The shelter owner, Maggie, had even asked about the model of my car, since modern vehicles used technology that wasn't allowed.

Trying to lighten the mood, I shot Izzy a smile. "At least the weather's nice and sunny."

Izzy gave a small murmur of agreement. She never spoke, because she had selective mutism due to an unthinkable childhood trauma—seeing her mother get shot when she was only four years old. Since her father was an initial suspect, she'd been placed into the foster system. By the time he was exonerated, he was unemployed and incapable of caring for his child, so she'd stayed in the system.

And yet we communicated well, even without words. Sometimes I thought I could hear her voice in my head, even though she hadn't spoken a full word since she was four. But over the past month or so, she'd taken to grunting and making sounds. I attributed that to her sessions with the school counselor, but the counselor said it was because Izzy knew she was safe with me, and that I wouldn't let her go back into the system without a fight.

She was definitely right about that. When Izzy and I had met at the library and I'd discovered she needed a new foster home, I'd moved heaven and earth to have her placed with me. From the get-go, Izzy felt like the daughter I'd never have, since I was thirty-six and didn't see marriage in my future.

As we rounded a curve, the farmhouse sprang into view. Izzy's eyes widened as she took it all in—

the sprawling white house, the chicken coop, the cows in the pasture, and the goats in their pen. There would be plenty to do during our time at the shelter, which I was euphemistically calling a "retreat."

A retreat from an unhinged stalker, more like.

A woman with long gray hair hurried down the front porch stairs toward Izzy's door. I rolled down the window, and she greeted us warmly.

"You must be Twila and Isabella." She clasped Izzy's hand, her gaze lingering for just a split-second on her turquoise bob and nose ring. "You're so welcome here. I'm Maggie Cooper, and my husband Walt is out feeding the cows." She gestured toward the fenced pasture. "But first, I have to ask, did y'all bring cell phones? We find it's best to keep them where you can't get to them, at least while you're with us. I know it's strict, but in this area, we have to keep to the rules of the National Radio Quiet Zone."

I obligingly pulled mine from my bag, powered it off, and handed it over. Izzy shot me a look, but followed suit. We'd known this was coming, but neither of us had really prepared for it.

Maggie gave a brisk nod. "I'm sure you're probably hungry. I was just setting out lunch for our ladies. If you want to park over beyond that red shed there"—she gestured toward a building—"you can come right on in and join us. Be sure to set your suitcases out, and Walt will grab them when he gets back."

As she turned toward the house, I pulled around to the spot she'd indicated. I headed out to grab the suitcases, giving Izzy some time to sit in silence. New people and situations often threw her into a tailspin, and I wanted to make this transition as easy as possible. Goodness knew she'd already had plenty of abrupt changes in her life.

A couple of orange striped barn cats slunk toward me, probably looking for food. The moment Izzy caught sight of them, she jumped out of the car.

Sensing the presence of a benevolent newcomer, they hurried toward her, rubbing around her legs. She crouched down, scratching behind their ears.

"You're a natural with them. Have you ever had a cat?" I asked.

She took a moment, then shrugged. If she'd been around cats, she didn't remember.

Grabbing my laptop bag and tote, I led the way toward the white picket fence enclosing the front yard. I swung the gate open to let Izzy in, sending the cats scurrying toward the barn.

We stopped, taking in the closer view of the house. It had two stories along with an attic level, and a long porch ran along the front. A gable had been built off the back, and enclosed, two-story porches ran the length of an extension on one side.

A small boy careened down the steps toward us, his black curls bouncing. He stretched chubby arms up to me as his liquid, dark eyes met mine.

His mother jogged over, apologizing as she scooped him up. "Darius! How many times I got to tell you, don't go runnin' out the door?" She gave me an apologetic nod. "He's five, and wild as wild. I'm Kenya, by the way."

I smiled. "I'm Twila, and this is my daughter Izzy." I'd taken to leaving the "foster" off, since it seemed unnecessary. I'd applied to adopt Izzy, so we just had to wait for the system to catch up with our plan.

"Nice to meet you, ladies." She set Darius down and nudged him back up the stairs. "Miss Maggie has lunch ready, hon. You head on in to the table." She grinned back at us and said, "It's hamburgers today. They got the best beef here, straight from their own cows."

I felt a flash of concern, since I'd notified Maggie that Izzy was a vegetarian. But as we followed Kenya inside and the dining room came into view, I realized we had nothing to worry about. Maggie had set out enough side dishes on the long table to feed an army. Some things didn't change, no matter where you were in West Virginia. I'd grown up in the south-western part of the state, where one church dinner could fill you up for hours. Maggie clearly adhered to the same standard.

Darius scrambled into his booster seat and started playing with his silverware. "Where should we wash our hands?" I asked Kenya.

She pointed to a nearby bathroom door, so Izzy and I headed in to wash up. When we came out, others were taking their seats. Maggie smiled and pointed to two chairs on the end. "Have yourself a seat, and we'll make our introductions."

Outside of Kenya, there were two other women staying at Cooper's Corner—Angel, who gave us a friendly smile, and Rae, who came across as disinterested. I shared a brief explanation of why we'd come, and Walt came in during the middle of it. The slim man washed up, then took a seat next to Maggie.

"Nice to meet you, Twila and Izzy. Now, what say we pray and eat some of this delicious food?" he suggested.

Maggie gave an approving nod. Once Walt finished praying, we started passing the food around. Izzy eagerly spooned good-sized helpings of pasta salad, fries, and coleslaw onto her plate. I was thankful she'd found plenty to eat.

As Angel passed the burgers my way, Maggie said, "You probably read this online, but everyone is expected to help with farm chores. There's nothing too strenuous—we just need help keeping this place running. We have a schedule up on the fridge. I noticed you liked the cats, Izzy, so I was thinking you could handle their feedings, if you want. Twila, I'd love some extra help with the laundry, if you wouldn't mind."

"That sounds perfect." Laundry wasn't my favorite chore, but I'd do anything to make sure Izzy was safe. "My job requires me to be online quite a bit —I know you said that was possible, but in a limited way. Could you show me how to do that?" I took a bite of my loaded burger, its taste exploding in my mouth. "This is wonderful," I added.

"Grass-fed beef," Walt explained. "I've been

breeding Black Angus for nigh on thirty years—I started when we moved to the farm. These are some of the fattest and most docile beefers you'll find."

Angel offered, "I'll show you how to connect to the satellite internet."

"Satellite connections are allowed in this area?" I asked.

"It's a trial run," Maggie explained. "The scientists are monitoring how much it'll interfere with their equipment at the observatory. They've extended the period a little, but we're still trying to be sparing with it. I told them about your computer job, and they said two to three hours a day should be okay."

That would be enough time for me to do my virtual assistant work for authors—including one of the top romantic suspense authors of our day, Alexandra Dubois. I couldn't drop the ball for Alex, because she'd just hired me, and there were plenty of other VAs who'd be more than happy to step into my shoes.

"They're not as strict in our zone," Walt said. "We're kind of on the outskirts."

"Gotcha." I took a bite of potato salad, and a burst of dill hit my tongue. "Delicious," I told Maggie.

She smiled. "I can tell we're going to get along just fine."

Rae abruptly shoved her chair back and stood. She shot me what could only be construed as a glare, and I felt Izzy recoil at my side.

"I'm heading out to feed the goats," Rae announced before stalking out of the room.

Once Rae's footsteps had faded, Maggie said quietly, "Rae might come off a bit harsh, but she's just wounded. Like Kenya and Angel, she's suffered greatly at the hands of someone who swore he loved her." She sighed. "I keep offering for her to meet with our friend in town who's a therapist, but she's not ready yet."

Kenya gave a snort. "That girl ain't never going to be ready."

Angel gave her hand a pat. "People can surprise you."

Kenya laughed. "Don't I know it. But not always for the good, honey."

Walt stood. "I'd best get back to work. I need to change the knives on my mower so I can start haying, soon as this next storm system passes."

"It's so dry," I said. "I'm sure you all could use the rain."

Maggie frowned. "Yes, but I start getting antsy when we have such a hot, dry June. When the rain finally does come, creeks and rivers can flood."

"I'm just happy you have AC in the house," Kenya said. "It'd be awful without it. I think it hit ninety yesterday when I was out weeding the garden. Poor Darius chugged two big bottles of lemonade."

The boy squealed at the mention of his name, shoving a fry into his mouth.

Maggie glanced at Izzy's empty plate and offered her more pasta salad, which Izzy gratefully accepted. I was glad to see there'd be an ample supply of food while we stayed, since it had been included in the cost. Although battered women could stay at Cooper's Corner free of charge, our layover here would eat up my entire emergency fund, and costs would continue to add up, depending on how long I decided to stay.

I glanced at Izzy, who looked tired. "We might take a little tour around, if that's okay," I said. "I could use some fresh air after that drive. But could we help with the dishes first?"

Angel shook her head. "I'm on kitchen duty today," she said kindly. "You two feel free to walk around."

"Just don't go all the way to the treeline past the goat area," Maggie said. "I keep my honeybee hives there."

I sucked in a breath. "That's a good thing you told me. I'm deathly allergic to beestings." When Izzy's eyebrows shot up, I hurried to add, "Don't worry—I brought my Epipen. I figured there'd be bees around a farm." I patted Izzy's hand. "It'll be fine."

TWO

The orange striped cats were back as we walked out of the front yard fence, and they brought friends. A few gray tabbies darted in front of us, effectively leading the way to the chicken coop. Izzy gave a start when the chickens fluttered up, but she was soon transfixed by their chaotic pecking. She shot me a concerned look, and I guessed what she was asking.

"I'm sure they've been fed already," I assured her. "Probably early this morning. I'm guessing that's someone's chore." I glanced around. "Rae said she's feeding the goats, so we can leave her to it. She didn't seem interested in chatting with us."

Izzy gave a small grunt of agreement, then gestured toward a dusty trail leading into the shaded woods.

"Good idea. That looks cooler, and it isn't the honeybee area Maggie was talking about," I said. "We could take a little walk, then head back."

Together, we plunged into the forest. The freshly greened-out oaks and maples provided a welcome relief from the heat. Ferns, hollies, and honeysuckle formed a thick underbrush beneath the tree canopy. Izzy stopped to examine a fallen log that was covered in lichen.

Just as I was about to join her, a man's voice drifted up from somewhere over the hillside to our left. "Help! Is someone out there?"

I froze. "Walt's outside somewhere, but that didn't sound like him."

Izzy gave me a worried look.

"Maybe some other men work on the farm," I reasoned out loud. "But the Coopers didn't mention anyone." I wasn't sure if I wanted to climb the hill and see who was on the other side. Women came to Cooper's Corner to find shelter from their abusers. What if one of them had tracked someone down? I didn't want to face anyone potentially violent on my own.

"How about this—I'll walk you back to the house. You can let Maggie know, while I try to find Walt." Izzy would write it down, alerting Maggie that a strange man was out in the woods.

But the man called out again. "I'm injured! Please help me!"

I hesitated. "Do you have your pepper spray?"

Izzy dug into the cargo pocket in her shorts, producing the pepper spray she never went without after the stalking incidents. She handed it over, understanding what I was going to do.

"I'm going to check things out. You head back to the house, okay? Just tell Maggie what's going on."

Izzy took off without hesitation. I started to climb the leaf-covered hill, dodging low tree branches and blackberry brambles. As I topped the ridge, a tall, muscular man came into view. He was lying in a more open area.

He propped himself up on one elbow and shouted, "Thank goodness! I've gotten a serious sprain—or maybe it's a break. I can't tell. I was out hiking and twisted my foot in a hole."

I came closer as he continued, keeping one hand on the pepper spray in my pocket.

"I kept going as long as I could, but my foot gave out here. I couldn't contact anyone since it's a radio silent zone. Probably a stupid place to hike, in retrospect."

He had a scruffy, dark blond beard and an unruly head of hair. A sleeve of tattoos ran up one arm. His observant hazel eyes reflected intelligence. And from the look of his exposed, swollen ankle, it was clear he wasn't lying.

"I'll get some help." I continued to keep my distance, just in case.

"I need to ice this as soon as I can. I've been lying here for over an hour now. Maybe I could roll over onto the tarp I brought, then you could drag me out of here. The tarp's in my backpack, if you wouldn't mind grabbing it."

I was five foot five and no string bean, but he looked to be over two hundred pounds of heavy muscle. "I'm not sure I could budge you," I said. "And I definitely can't pull you up that hill."

He chuckled. "Honesty—I like that. And you're probably right. I'm happy to wait, but please hurry. Pain's been shooting through my ankle, and I didn't pack any ibuprofen. My name's Jude, by the way."

I nodded without introducing myself. As I scrambled up the hill, my thoughts whirled. How far did the Coopers' property extend? Did it butt up against woodland where the public was free to roam? That seemed unlikely. Yet Jude's backpack seemed to attest to his claim he'd been hiking.

As I emerged from the woods, Walt zoomed up on his four-wheeler. "Maggie told me there's some man out here?" he asked.

"He's over that hill." I pointed the way. "He said his name is Jude, and that he sprained his ankle. Do you know him?"

Walt shook his head. "Never heard of 'im." Without another word, he revved up and peeled off toward the incline. I hesitated, unsure whether to return to the farmhouse or to help Walt.

My question was answered when Rae jogged toward me. "Maggie sent me to help Walt and you," she said. "Izzy told her someone was injured."

"She's right. He's over this way." I took off toward the hill, with Rae close behind. She didn't say a word until we topped the steep rise, where she stopped short, staring at the man Walt was trying to boost onto his one good foot. He'd probably planned to get him on the four-wheeler, but Jude had at least sixty pounds on the wiry Walt, so it wasn't a fast process.

Feeling the waves of anxiety rolling off Rae, I asked, "Is something wrong?"

She let out a breath. "No. I just needed to be sure he wasn't...well, one of ours." She headed toward the men, and I followed. She hadn't meant "one of ours" in a good way, that was for sure.

Jude glanced over as we approached, one arm awkwardly draped around Walt's neck. "Thank you. I didn't get your names."

"I'm Twila," I said.

"Rae." Her blunt answer shut down any further chitchat. She stepped closer, wrapping Jude's other arm around her neck. Together, she and Walt started moving Jude toward the machine.

As he limped alongside the four-wheeler, I helped him ease onto the seat. Once he'd leaned on the handlebars, Walt and I managed to lift his bum foot over the seat.

"I'll sit right in front of you and drive you to the house," Walt offered. "It's tricky enough maneuvering up that hill, and I doubt you'd want to take it on in your state."

"I'd appreciate that," Jude said.

"I'll grab your backpack," I offered, hoisting it onto my shoulder. The green canvas pack was surprisingly light. Jude must've drunk all the water he'd packed.

Once Jude had thanked me, Walt assured him,

"Maggie'll have you fixed up in no time." He started the engine and eased toward the hill.

Rae led me back to the house, setting a fast pace. I guessed she was five-foot-ten, at least, and built like an Amazon. It was a wonder to me that someone had ever attempted to harm her, but abusers were no respecters of persons, I supposed.

It drove home the reality of what Cooper's Corner was here for—to protect women who found themselves in a situation they'd never planned on. Women like me and like Izzy.

JUDE HAD COLLAPSED onto the couch by the time we got back, so Walt must've managed to help him up the porch steps. His ankle was already wrapped and propped on a floral velvet pillow, and Maggie was handing him ibuprofen as I walked past. Angel was close behind her, offering a glass of lemonade and a sandwich, which Jude received with profuse thanks.

Izzy was keeping Darius busy with blocks in the dining room, and Kenya wasn't around, so I assumed she was out doing a chore.

I took a closer look at Jude's ankle, which was still ballooned out, even with the wrapping. "Do you have an ice pack?" I asked Maggie. "It's way too swollen."

"I agree, it is. I keep meaning to buy one of those gel packs, but still haven't gotten one. There's a big bag of peas in the garage freezer, though. You could grab those."

After some searching, I managed to find the peas, which I wrapped in a kitchen towel. I gently draped them over Jude's foot.

His eyes caught mine. "I can't thank you enough for coming when I called. I think I was getting dehydrated."

"I guessed you'd drunk all your water supply," I said.

He nodded, and I noted the dust coating his cheekbones. He really needed to get cleaned up, but how was he going to manage that?

Maggie said, "I've seen some broken bones in my time, and I don't think your ankle's broken, given how it looks. Plus, you can still move it. It's probably a severe sprain. You definitely have a lot of bruising —you twisted it up good."

He gave a pained grin. "My new hiking boots really let me down. They didn't stabilize my ankle one bit."

"You're not going to be getting up and down the stairs anytime soon," Maggie warned. "I'll let you sleep in our son Adam's room downstairs. He moved out long ago, but there are still some rock band posters up on the walls and high school things around. I try to keep things tidy, but I've hesitated to throw things away. Who knows what might be valuable someday, you know?"

Using his other foot to raise his pillow a bit, Jude said, "That'll be fine."

Maggie's lips twisted. "Those singers wear all black, and some of the men wear eyeliner. I think Adam called them indie singers. I never did get it."

Jude's eyes flicked my way, and I caught the twinkle in them. We were probably just a little older than her son, so we were familiar with the indie movement.

"Thanks for letting me know," he said solemnly.

I turned to the dining room, trying to hide my amused smile. Darius knocked Izzy's block tower down, then did a happy little jig. Her natural connection with children always encouraged me—they could understand each other without speaking a word.

Given that Jude seemed well taken care of, I said, "I might go do my internet work right now, if that's okay?"

Maggie nodded. "Of course. Angel can set you up. She's in the kitchen, I think."

I headed into the spacious, sunny kitchen, where Angel was busy chopping cabbage. "I'm working on slaw to go with the fried fish tonight. But I'll be making a special quinoa dish for Izzy, since she doesn't eat fish, right?"

"Right. She'll appreciate that."

"Good." She dropped her voice. "So, what do you make of Mister Tall, Mysterious, and Handsome in there?"

I gave a half-shrug. "He says he was hiking nearby, then he twisted his ankle and managed to make it into the Coopers' woods. He seems nice enough."

She nodded, turning back to her coleslaw prep. "It's still kind of weird, isn't it, to be hiking in this heat? The grass is so dry, it's almost crunchy. It's a nasty June for outdoor things."

She seemed a bit nervous, so I tried to reassure her. "Rae said he had no connection with any of you all. Otherwise, I wouldn't have suggested Walt bring him back to the house."

Angel flipped her pale blonde bangs out of her eyes. "Oh, of course. Don't worry about it. I'm oversensitive, hypervigilant, and a whole host of things, thanks to my ex. I tend to read into things."

I gave her an understanding nod, watching as she mixed mayo into the slaw. "Once you finish the slaw, would you have a spare minute to hook me up to the internet?" I asked. "That way I can do a little work."

She dusted her hands on a towel. "I can help you now. Kenya's upstairs, changing sheets, so I'll ask her if she can finish the food prep and I'll do her job. We swap chores pretty often around here, so don't be afraid to ask."

"I won't." As we passed through the dining room, I spoke to Izzy. "I'm going to get set up for the internet, but Kenya should be coming down soon, if you need help."

Izzy's cheeks dimpled as she grinned, a clear sign she was having fun. Darius had fallen silent, intent on stacking his tower as high as he possibly could.

Angel and I walked by Jude, who seemed to be drifting off to sleep. Maggie and Walt were standing in the entryway, speaking in low voices. As I reached the staircase landing, I heard Walt say, "We can't keep him here long. I'm not buying his story."

THREE

Jude moved onto the bed in Adam's old room, so Angel brought his supper in on a tray that night. The rest of us sat at the table, enjoying fried fish and potatoes. Angel had done a great job taking Izzy's vegetarian needs into consideration, providing a quinoa dish with fresh herbs and two other vegetable options.

Rae didn't seem inclined to talk over supper, but Kenya was eager to interact. "Maggie said you're not here for the same reason we are." Her phrasing was delicate, probably out of respect for Darius' listening ears. "You work for authors, she said?"

I warmed to the subject. "Yes. I have a background in English and marketing, so designing graphics and setting up ad campaigns comes pretty naturally for me."

Kenya's eyes shone. "I love reading. Darius and I spend a lot of time at the library, because it's so peaceful. You work for any big authors I might know?"

Alex had told me she didn't mind if I shared that she employed me, since any publicity was good publicity. Unfortunately, she'd learned that the hard way a couple of years ago, when a crazed stalker fan had followed her to a secluded cabin and nearly killed her. Her ordeal had been all over the news for months, but her readers banded together to show their support, and as a result, her book sales had broken even more records. "There's one name you might recognize," I said. "Alexandra Dubois. She writes the *Lipstick and Lies* series."

Kenya whistled. "Get *out!* She's one of my favorite authors. Can you tell her that?"

I smiled, unsurprised by her reaction. "I will."

She looked concerned. "I hope she's recovered after that insane attack. That must've knocked her for a loop."

I dipped a bite of fish into my tartar sauce. "She's been doing well. I don't know if you saw, but she's working on a new series."

Kenya's eyes widened, and she gave an eager little clap.

Clearly unconcerned about what Alexandra Dubois might be doing next, Rae leveled an accusatory stare at me. "So, why are you really here?"

Izzy gaped, and Maggie's eyebrows raised. "Rae," she scolded.

I waved a dismissive hand. Rae clearly wanted to stir the pot, but I had no compunction about telling her the truth. "Some man was stalking Izzy at school. They still haven't caught him."

Rae had the decency to look disturbed. "Oh, I'm sorry. I didn't realize."

I wanted to say, "No, you didn't," but I restrained myself and took a bite of green beans.

Angel walked in from the kitchen. "Jude said thanks for the food, and that it looks delicious."

Maggie flashed Walt an unreadable look. "Thanks for taking his meal to him. Did he need any more ibuprofen or ice?" she asked.

"I brought him a fresh bag of frozen corn. But it might be a good idea to buy a bigger ice pack in town tomorrow."

I spoke up. "Were you planning to take him to urgent care or anything?"

"We'll see how he's doing in the morning," Maggie said. "I'm pretty sure it's a sprain, so he'll need to keep it wrapped and stay off it a while. Our son Adam had a couple of breaks, and they were far worse from the get-go."

I wasn't sure if that was the best plan of action, since Jude had seemed to be in considerable pain. But it wasn't my place to interfere in his care, since I, too, was a guest at Cooper's Corner. Besides, Walt didn't seem to want Jude sticking around. He'd probably drive him into town at his earliest convenience.

Darius popped a ketchup-drenched fried potato into his mouth. "Mm," he said, smacking his lips.

Maggie looked at me. "Thanks for getting all

those beds made. Were you able to get your computer work done, by the way?"

"I was—thanks for asking. I got all my emails sent and my business done for the day."

Izzy made a hand signal for time passing. Guessing at her request, I asked Maggie, "Did you have anything else planned for tonight? It's been a pretty eventful day, so we might just relax in our room, if you don't mind."

"Oh, of course. Please do," Maggie said. "You probably saw the bookshelves at the top of the stairs. Feel free to help yourself to our books while you're here. We get a lot of book donations, so there's a little of everything." She turned to Izzy. "What do you like to read, hon?"

When Izzy gave her a shy smile, Maggie clapped a hand to her mouth. "Oh my goodness, I forgot she doesn't talk."

"That's an easy mistake to make. Izzy's very communicative, even without words." I was used to this kind of disconnect. Izzy had thrived in school because of her ability to make people forget her muteness.

"I can tell you have a special bond." Angel spoke softly, but her words carried a soothing balm.

"I'm planning to adopt Izzy soon," I explained. "She's spent too many years in foster care."

Maggie released a happy sigh. "Well, isn't that wonderful?" She stood, stacking a few dirty plates. "We also have cookies for dessert, if y'all want any. I used my mother's chocolate chip cookie recipe."

Darius grinned, his eyes widening.

"Just one, little man," his mom cautioned. "Your bedtime is coming up soon."

It must be such a reprieve for Kenya to be in a place where she didn't have to worry about feeding and protecting her son. I'd found myself breathing easier at our mountain hideaway, too.

But every now and then, I worried that if someone could track Izzy down at her private school, would it be at all difficult to find her here, too?

Appreciative of the mental silence afforded by our limited internet, Izzy and I chose books to unwind with. I recommended she try *And Then There Were None* by Agatha Christie, while I pulled out my copy of the latest book in the *Hunger Games* series. It seemed a reversal of what we should be reading at our ages, but I was a fan of dystopian books, while Izzy preferred mysteries. She curled up on the chintz couch, allowing me to stretch out on the canopy bed.

I opened to my bookmarked spot. Just as I was finding my place, my phone rang from the night-stand, jarring me. I'd forgotten I'd connected it to the satellite internet. I hurried to pick it up.

A sweetly Southern voice sounded on the other end. "Twila? It's me, Shana."

It was Izzy's CPS worker. Why would she be calling me here? Had they found the stalker?

"Hi, Shana, what's up?"

"I'm sorry to bother you, but I didn't want to text since you have limited internet. Listen, something's come up in our DHHR office that I think you should be aware of."

I tried to steel myself. "Okay, go on."

"Someone remotely hacked into our records—in particular, into *Izzy's* records—last week. It was just before you headed up there."

"What are you saying?" I kept my voice quiet, trying not to alarm Izzy.

"Unfortunately, it means that whoever got into the system knows where you are. I had already submitted your temporary address form, as I'm required to do."

I stayed silent, unwilling to put my fears into words. The hacker was likely one and the same with Izzy's school stalker. What kind of a relentless maniac were we dealing with here?

I glanced at Izzy, who was absently twirling a strand of turquoise hair. She looked like she was lost in her book, but I suspected she was listening to every word I said. She had a curious mind, like I did.

"We've referred the incident for investigation, but I'm not sure how long it'll take to get answers," Shana continued. "Do you want to move somewhere else? I can get you some shelter names up that way."

That was definitely something I'd have to consider. Even though we'd just settled in, if the stalker was already on his way, we couldn't risk staying.

But moving again might present the same problem. "You'd have to enter our new address in the system, wouldn't you?" I asked.

She sighed. "I'm supposed to, but that wouldn't be safe. I'll talk with my supervisor and see if I could just keep the address in my lockbox at home. That way it would be recorded, but I'd be the only one who could access it. And I could contact the DHHR office in whatever county you moved to and alert them personally. Whatever county you wind up in has to schedule a worker to make monthly checks, same as you have here."

I couldn't wait to get Izzy out of the system that played Big Brother, nosing into practically every detail of our lives. Yet I understood the necessity of checks and balances to flush out neglectful foster parents. Izzy had been placed in a home like that. Thankfully, her CPS worker had recognized something wasn't right within a couple of visits. She had promptly reported the parents and moved Izzy.

Now we were forced to trust that Shana would manage to protect us from afar. Sometimes foster care felt like a succession of exercises designed to prove you have no semblance of control.

"Sure, I understand," I said finally. "You can text me the names and addresses of any nearby places, since I have satellite internet. I'll check into them. In the meantime, I'll keep Izzy close." I turned a falsely reassuring smile toward my daughter, but she was still pretending to read.

Shana's tone was gentle. "I'm so sorry this happened. It truly shouldn't have."

After she said goodbye, I walked over to Izzy, dreading how the news would make her feel. She'd had more than her fair share of shocks in her life. When would it ever end?

But she closed her book, bravely meeting my worried gaze. As I told her what was going on, she slouched against the couch, making herself small. Her counselor had told me that there were actually four trauma responses—fight, flight, freeze, or fawn, and Izzy had always chosen flight. It's what had kept her alive when her mother was murdered—she'd hidden in the hall closet so quietly, the killer had been unaware of her presence.

"You'll need to stay in my sight, as long as we're here," I said. "I'm sorry to have to do that, but if someone's hiding nearby, I can't let you venture off too far. I'll explain things to Maggie, and I'm sure she'll understand. I'll tell her you can do chores tomorrow, but I'll need to accompany you. I'll check into new places for us to stay, and we'll move as soon as there's a room available."

Izzy's downcast look told me she was tired of bouncing around like a pinball, but we had no other alternative. If someone was tracking her, we couldn't stay here like sitting ducks.

Once we'd read for awhile, I finally turned the lock on our door and shoved a chair under the knob, like I'd seen in the movies. After retrieving Izzy's pepper spray, I placed it on the nightstand. Izzy gave a slow blink, but curled up and rolled over, pulling the white comforter up to her chin. The air conditioning was quite chilly, but I had no idea how to turn it down.

I gave her a brief hug before tucking myself deeper under the comforter. Sharing a bed wasn't ideal, but tonight, I was grateful for our close quarters. I might not get any sleep to speak of, but I planned to be Izzy's first line of defense, live or die.

FOUR

In the morning, I headed straight for the kitchen to talk with Maggie, who was slinging eggs and bacon like she worked at a diner. Her eyes widened as I told her someone had hacked into Izzy's files and might try to follow us here.

"I won't have either one of you worrying about chores," she said, shaking her spatula in the air.

"We want to do something, though." I picked up the tray she'd prepared for Jude. "The least I can do is help out inside. I'll join you on kitchen duty, and Izzy can handle the cats. It's not far to the barn, and I'll go with her."

She hesitated. "I'll let you pitch in, but you have to promise to tell Walt or me if you have any worries at all. Out here in the country, we have all kinds of ways of dealing with threats." She gave me a serious nod.

"I will. Now, I'll take this to Jude for you," I said. "How's he doing today, do you know?"

She flipped bacon, backing away as hot grease splattered the stovetop. Turning the burner down, she said, "He hasn't come out yet, so I'm not sure if he's able to move around. Let me know if he needs anything."

"I will."

I walked past Izzy, who was helping Rae set the table. To my surprise, Rae was keeping up a steady stream of largely one-sided conversation. She seemed to have warmed to our presence here.

With the tray balanced against my hip, I gave Jude's door a quick rap.

"Come in." His voice was muffled.

I twisted the knob and stepped into the large room. The damp air smelled fresh, and since the bathroom door was still shut, I figured Jude had just showered.

"Jude? I brought your breakfast," I called out. "I'll set it on the far side of your bed." That way he could easily sit and eat.

"Thanks. Sorry it's taking me so long to get out of here—it's hard to get my jeans on over this swollen ankle. Everything's taking a while."

"That's okay." I idly straightened a couple of older Jack Reacher novels on his nightstand. "Maggie wondered if you needed anything. I'd be glad to bring some ibuprofen, or maybe a bag of frozen vegetables for your ankle." Catching sight of a yellowed, cut-out newspaper article tucked under the bottom book, I skimmed the headline. My stomach instantly clenched as I read, "Local Mother Brutally Slain in her Home."

I pushed the book aside, only to find the exact photo I'd expected to see. Shana had shared the same article with me when I'd signed up to foster Izzy. The blurry photo featured three-year-old Izzy in her fluffy Easter dress, smiling from ear to ear in her father's arms. Her mother stood next to them, gaze fixed on her child.

The bathroom doorknob turned, so I hastily covered the tragic clipping with the book and whirled to greet Jude, a smile plastered on my face. I was able to fake friendliness when needed, and it was definitely needed now.

Jude had crutches tucked under both arms, and he haltingly made his way toward the bed. "Maggie found these in her son's closet. They're a little short, but at least they keep me moving in the same direction. You can tell her I'm doing a little better, since the pain isn't so sharp. I plan to keep my ankle up today."

He wore a clean white V-neck tee, and he'd made an effort to comb his thick hair and beard. He stretched his tattooed arm out to touch the bed, then eased onto the mattress with a groan. Throwing a glance at the food, he said, "Please tell Maggie that I appreciate everything. I'm hoping the swelling will go way down by tomorrow."

A sudden, searing anxiety filled me. I didn't want Jude hanging around the farm—not even for a day. My daughter's photo was sitting on his nightstand.

He might've been the one who'd accessed her records.

"I could drive you into urgent care in town," I suggested. "It's no problem. It would probably put Maggie's mind at ease. I think you need medical attention, since your ankle's still swollen."

His lips quirked beneath his beard, and his sharp eyes met mine. I got the distinct feeling he could see right through my desperate attempt to get him away from the house, but it was the only way I could be sure he'd be nowhere near Izzy. I could use his exam time to check online for an available shelter room. Then, once I got back, Izzy and I could slip out. Maggie and Walt would understand our haste to move on.

"Okay, sure. If you think so." He sounded like he was humoring me. Had he guessed I was blowing smoke?

"I'll let Maggie know," I said. "We can head out after breakfast cleanup is done." I'd have Izzy lock herself in our room until I returned.

"Thanks." He turned, sliding his tray closer. "If you don't mind, I'll go ahead and eat."

"Of course." I backed out, pulling the door closed behind me. As I walked into the dining room, I let out a sigh. I needed to get us out of this situation sooner rather than later. Izzy's information had been hacked last week, which gave Jude plenty of time to travel here. Had he intentionally injured himself, hoping to gain access to the house?

If so, he was downright psychotic.

We were digging into our breakfast when Walt walked in, looking worried. He headed straight for the bathroom.

Maggie spoke sharply, pulling him up short. "Walt, your boots!"

He dropped his gaze to his boots, as if just realizing he'd tracked dirt across the living room rug. He started pulling them off. "Sorry, hon. Problem is, that sky out there isn't looking right." He walked toward the picture window and pushed the lacy curtain aside. "It's getting yellower by the minute. Were they calling for tornados or something?"

"Just storms," Angel said. "Maybe severe."

"I'm reminded of that 2012 derecho." Walt seemed lost in reflection. "The sky looked the same then, and the cows were restless like they are today. That's why I hightailed it back to the house. Is everyone inside?"

Maggie's face blanched, but she glanced around. "They are. Jude's still in his room, I believe."

Before she could explain more, an incessant wind pressed against the front of the house. Loud cracks sounded outside, followed by heavy thuds. Trees and limbs must be hitting the ground. I shoved my chair back, shooting Izzy a look to follow my lead.

"Get into the basement!" Maggie screeched. She jumped up, leading the way to a small door tucked under the stairs. Kenya snatched Darius up and followed close behind her. Izzy and I fell into line next, and then Angel and Rae.

Walt said, "I'll get Jude." He pounded off to the bedroom.

We'd just made it down the basement stairs when the electricity went out, blanketing us in thick darkness. Izzy reached out and clung to my hand in the cool, damp space.

Walt flung the basement door open, allowing rays of sunlight to beam downstairs. "It's already over," he said. "Sure enough, it was another derecho. We lost three of our pines out front."

I heard a gasp in the dark, and Maggie said, "I knew we should've gotten them cut after that last one."

I wasn't sure where the other ladies had lived before, but the very word "derecho" struck fear into the heart of every West Virginian who'd been in the state in 2012, when the first one hit. The straight-line windstorm had torn through trees like butter, collapsed buildings, and knocked out power lines. Some people had gone without electricity for over ten days, due to the logistics of repairs along the precarious sides of the Appalachian mountains. We could only hope the damage wasn't as extensive this time.

"Y'all can come on up," Walt continued. "I didn't even manage to get Jude into the basement before it was all over."

"I'm okay," Jude chimed in, propping his big frame against the open door. He'd only managed to get one crutch under him.

"We're going to have to check out the damage," Walt said. "I'd take Jude with me, but..."

Rae spoke into the darkness. "I'll help." She eased around me and cautiously walked up the stairs.

As Rae reached the door, Walt said, "Okay. I'd like the rest of you to stay around the house until we can get a handle on things. We might have some cows out or power lines down. I'll take a walkie-talkie to stay in touch with you, Maggie."

"I'll be listening," Maggie assured him. "Let's head upstairs, everyone."

As Rae and Walt headed out, Angel turned on her phone light, beaming it toward the stairs so we could all see as we walked up. Jude maintained his vigilant stance near the basement door, as if offering moral support.

"Thanks, Angel." Maggie gripped the railing as she eased up the stairs. "Just be sure to turn your light off as soon as everyone's out. We'll need to conserve all the battery power we can."

Since I'd experienced the last derecho stuck in an apartment with no electricity, I was only too aware of how precious our remaining battery life was. Thankfully, my laptop was fully charged, so if the satellite connection still worked, I'd shoot a message to my author Alex, explaining why I'd have to be offline until power was restored.

Jude finally shuffled toward the couch as I topped the stairs and pulled the door closed behind me. I wished I could warn Izzy about the news article I'd found in his room, but I couldn't possibly do that here. Everyone was uneasy and anxious, including little Darius, who had fallen uncharacteristically silent as his mom rocked him in her arms.

Maggie made a beeline for a walkie-talkie sitting on a charger base. She pushed a button, and it crackled to life.

Jude gave her a curious look. "You're allowed to use that in the radio quiet zone?"

Maggie nodded. "Our area allows for their use in emergencies, and this definitely qualifies as one. After the last derecho, we bought these long-range walkie-talkies with battery backup."

Uncertain what to do next, I took a seat at the table. Izzy followed me, leaning over to give me a silent hug.

I gave both her arms a reassuring squeeze. "It's going to be okay," I whispered.

Walt's walkie-talkie voice suddenly rattled through the room. "A tree came down on the pasture fence. Rae and I are going to fix it. I haven't checked up the driveway yet, but there are no downed lines by the house, so you should be okay working around there if you need to."

"Roger that." Maggie carefully placed the walkie-talkie on the coffee table, like it was some separate entity.

I had to grin at her terminology. "Is there anything I could do to help?" I offered.

She blinked, as if waking from a nightmare. "I'm trying to recall tricks we learned from the last derecho. We have an outdoor fire pit, so if you want to start a fire and cook up the meat I've thawed in the fridge, that would be good. We'll leave the freezer meats where they are for the time being, but as the days go on, we'll have to pull those out and grill them up, too." She groaned. "And we're still on well water. That was our biggest issue last time. We've tried to get the water company to hook us up to their supply, but they don't want to dig a line all the way down our long drive. That means we'll have to haul water to the animals, since their watering troughs have already gotten low after this dry spell."

"I'll help with the water," Kenya offered. "Izzy or Angel, would you mind looking after Darius? I'd rather keep him inside, out of the heat."

Angel said, "Sure," and Izzy bobbed her head in agreement.

I hadn't really wanted us to stay another day with Jude around, but now we had no choice. The narrow, winding drive to town would doubtless be a complete mess at this point.

The truth was, Izzy and I were trapped, so I'd have to keep an eye on Jude at all times. I regretted coming to his aid in the first place, but I couldn't have ignored an injured hiker begging for help.

Maybe I could force him into some kind of confession as to why he had the article on Izzy, but what then? Maggie and Walt might demand he leave, but then someone would have to drive him into town, which was likely an impossibility right now.

"We'll shift all the outdoor chores to early morning and late evening since it's too hot during the day," Maggie continued. "And we'll need to conserve water."

"Do we have enough bottled water on hand to get through a few days?" Angel asked.

Maggie nodded. "That's one thing we did do after the last derecho. We got some donations and stocked a whole room in our basement with bottled water. We should be okay for a good while."

That was good news. Deciding it was best not to delay my task, I said, "I'll get the fire pit going. Where's your lighter?"

Maggie led me into the kitchen, and I threw a parting glance at Jude, who had propped his injured foot up on the coffee table. It was still noticeably swollen, and he was probably experiencing a good deal of pain with it.

Izzy followed my glance. Without a word, she walked into the kitchen and came out with a large bag of frozen corn. She pressed it onto Jude's ankle with a tentative smile.

I stiffened. That smile was one Izzy didn't offer easily. It was one that told me she trusted Jude, and I couldn't allow her to do that.

"Will you help me with the fire?" I asked her.

My tone must've sounded far too severe, because every head in the room turned my way. Jude's gaze snapped to me.

But Izzy read the warning in my words, and she immediately came to my side. Angel would have to look after Darius, because I needed to keep an eye on my own daughter.

FIVE

After some effort, Izzy and I managed to get a nice fire going, then we positioned the cast iron skillet on the grill rack to cook some chicken cutlets Maggie had thawed.

We retreated into the shade of the porch as the meat sizzled. Since we were alone, I decided to take the opportunity to explain why I had serious misgivings about Jude.

Izzy's brow furrowed as I told her about the news article in Jude's room. She shook her head, disbelieving.

"I know he seems nice, but I need you to stay away from him," I said. "And I'm not sure how long we'll be here, anyway. I'd planned to leave today, but now it's not looking too promising that we can get out of here."

She shook her head again, frustrated.

"You don't want to leave?" I asked.

"Nnn." She was making a serious effort to say "No."

"You're enjoying it here?"

She nodded, making a sweeping gesture encompassing the house, barn, and woods.

"It is peaceful. But now we have no electricity, so it'll get way too peaceful. No air conditioning or fans; no running water." I cringed. "I don't know how we'll even use the bathroom or clean up. What if this goes on for over a week, like last time?"

Izzy shrugged, taking the hair elastic from her wrist to pull her hair back into a tiny ponytail. These were not the kinds of issues she wanted to worry about, and I understood that. I was the mom here—that was *my* job.

I jumped up to take out the browned chicken. After setting it on a plate, I poured some sun-melted butter into the pan and added the remaining cutlets. "We'll figure it out," I said, with far more certainty than I felt.

RAE AND WALT returned about three hours later, dirty and sweaty after their efforts to secure the pasture fenceline. Angel hurried to bring them glasses of lukewarm lemonade from the fridge, adding a couple of already-melting ice cubes. Kenya had returned from her chores, as well, so Maggie and I transferred our hodgepodge lunch of fried chicken and peanut butter and jelly sandwiches to the table.

Jude rested on the couch, looking thoroughly uncomfortable. He'd propped up his leg as high as it could go on three stacked pillows.

Walt gulped down his lemonade before gruffly announcing, "The damage is extensive. I pushed a couple of downed limbs off the drive with my skid steer bucket, but there are several others that could snap off anytime." He threw a regretful look at Jude. Manual labor was definitely needed in this situation, and, even though Rae was strong, Jude would most certainly be stronger. His tall, muscular frame seemed tailor-made for hard work—far more than Walt's thin build.

Jude got the message. "I'm sorry, Walt. I promise you I'll be out there the moment my ankle gets strong enough to bear weight. I might be able to manage the four-wheeler at some point, so let me know if I can help with that."

Walt gave a quiet nod, taking his place at the table. During our meal, Maggie and Walt went over the logistics of life without running water and electricity, which didn't seem quite as bad as I'd anticipated. The only issue would be transporting enough water to the bathroom so that it could be poured into the tank to facilitate a flush. We could wash with rags and cold water for the time being, and the well had a hand pump, so more water could be brought up as needed.

"To light your rooms at night, you all are welcome to pull up those solar lights lining the sidewalk. We've bought plenty over the years, and all you have to do is put them outside each morning to charge them up again. It's a little trick we learned during the last derecho," Maggie explained.

It was brilliant. I felt better knowing we wouldn't have to rely on our phone flashlights, which would undoubtedly die if this ordeal went on for long.

I finished off my chicken and started stacking the paper plates. At least we didn't have to worry about doing dishes, since Maggie also had a good supply of disposable utensils, plates, and cups. Rae stood and followed me into the kitchen, even though she wasn't on duty.

"Twila," she said, then stopped. My name sounded strange coming from her lips, since she barely knew me. "This is a weird question, but you said someone was stalking your daughter outside her school, right? And I'm assuming they didn't catch the guy?"

My stomach clenched. What was she getting at?

"That's right." I stuffed the plates into the trash can, then pulled out the bag and tied it off. I didn't see any reason to go into more detail, because there was hardly anything to share. A man in an old black car had been spotted outside the school several days in a row, sitting where Izzy would wait for me to pick her up. One day, he'd driven closer and tried to ask Izzy something. She'd done the wise thing and raced into the school office. When the police asked her for a description, she couldn't give one, since the man's hair had been tucked into a cap, and sunglasses had obscured his facial features.

Rae absently grabbed a carrot stick from the bowl on the counter and started munching on it. Around her mouthful, she said, "Was there some reason he targeted her, do you know?"

I hardly saw how it was any of her business. Why was she so curious about Izzy? "We don't know anything for certain," I said shortly.

She seemed to pick up on my tone. "I'm sorry. I just got to thinking, would he be the type to try and follow her here? I want to help you watch out for her." She dropped her voice. "I have a daughter, too. About Izzy's age, actually. Her dad's family got custody...it's a long story, but I recently got clean, so his parents were the safest ones for her to stay with. He doesn't have any contact with her, given his record of abuse. But I'm always worried he'll wriggle his way in and wreck her life, like he did mine."

I appreciated her opening up to me, since it helped me better understand her motivations. "Did you come here to recover?" I asked.

She nodded. "I had to get away from him and all my dealers at home. My plan is to prove I'm clean for good, then I want to build a real relationship with my daughter. My ex's parents have been really supportive."

Angel walked in with more bowls of raw veggies. She gave us a polite nod before focusing on transferring the food into plastic bags.

"That sounds hopeful," I said quietly.

Once Angel had finished her work, Rae said, "I'll be out and about with Walt for the rest of the day, since I prefer to stay outdoors. I'll keep my eyes open for anything—or anyone—out of place."

I released a long breath, thankful to have someone else looking out for Izzy. "Thank you."

Before I could ask what she thought of Jude, Izzy walked in. Rae took a step toward the dining room, but I stopped her by saying, "Izzy, Rae wants to help us. She's going to be keeping an eye out for you."

Rae awkwardly met Izzy's curious gaze. "I have a daughter, too," she explained.

Izzy smiled, as if it made perfect sense. And in some way, it did. Even though Rae had been hostile toward us when we arrived, she'd realized what a vulnerable situation Izzy was in right now, and she'd stepped up to help. I wouldn't forget her kindness while we were stuck at Cooper's Corner.

THE HOUSE GOT sweltery as the day wore on. Our trips to cook on the grill brought a welcome breath of fresh air, even though we had to keep the fire stoked.

"At least we have an unlimited supply of fresh eggs," I said. "Kenya said the chickens are laying up a storm. Maybe you could offer to make omelets some night for supper—I know how much you like those."

Izzy blinked her acknowledgement, idly using a spatula to prod a hamburger patty. Even though she disliked meat in general, she'd learned to cook it when the need arose.

A car approached on the front drive, so I walked

to the side of the house to see who was coming. Maybe emergency services were checking on people after the derecho? That would make sense in a rural area like this, where residents were largely cut off from communication. Izzy sidled up behind me, watching.

The SUV pulled to a stop by the picket fence, and a man stepped out. He had a dark beard, and he wore a polo shirt and jeans. After giving the place a once-over, he headed toward the gate and opened it, then made his way toward the front stairs. I considered intercepting him, but decided it would be best to view him from a safer distance, inside the house.

Determined to keep Izzy in my sight, I suggested, "Why don't you come into the kitchen with me and we'll see who he is."

Just as we entered the back door, the doorbell rang. Maggie rushed out of the laundry room to open it, and I saw her speaking with the stranger. After a few moments' conversation, she turned and asked, "Is Twila around?"

Stunned, I turned to Izzy. "You stay here unless I ask for you—maybe over in that far corner where you'll be out of sight."

Her blue eyes were wide, but she nodded agreement. I moved out into the open, making my way past the dining room table and into the living room, where the man was standing.

"This is Colin...what's your last name again?" Maggie asked.

"Meissner." He smiled at me. "I'm here to conduct

a home visit for Isabella, since I'll be her case worker in this county. Shana let me know she's settled here now, so I'm here for the initial visit and to set up a schedule. Sorry it was today, of all days. You all doing okay after that windstorm?"

Jude's room door opened, and he came out, crutches under his arms. After throwing a glance at Colin, he headed for the bathroom. I found this strange, since he had a bathroom in his room, but maybe he didn't have enough water to flush.

Colin must not have touched base with Shana since yesterday, when I'd talked to her about moving. But I didn't want to bring that up in front of everyone. To divert attention, I asked, "How are the roads? Did a lot of trees come down?"

Angel came in the back door, fresh eggs in hand. She glanced toward the corner where Izzy was, then looked out at us. I gave her a warning glance.

"Traveling is slow going," he said. "I was afraid a tree was going to fall on my vehicle coming up the drive. Power lines and trees are down across the whole state, so they're having to bring in outside crews to help. It'll be a slow process, I'm afraid. But since I promised Shana I'd drop in, I wanted to give it my best shot." He glanced toward the kitchen. "Do you have enough food and supplies?"

Maggie jumped in to assure him of what they'd stocked up on, so I let my attention wander back to Jude. He had emerged from the bathroom, only to prop himself up next to his bedroom door. It was obvious he was listening to every word Colin said, which made me a little panicky. He didn't need to know one more detail about Izzy.

I stepped closer to Colin. "Maybe we could talk somewhere more private," I suggested quietly. "You could join me on the front porch."

He gave me a quizzical look, but agreed, following me out the screen door. As we sat down on rocking chairs, I said, "You mentioned speaking with Shana, but she didn't say anything about you on the phone yesterday. Would you mind showing me some kind of credentials?" I figured I couldn't be too careful.

"Oh, certainly," he said. "I apologize that I didn't do that first thing." After rifling through papers on his clipboard, he handed me one that had his name listed as case worker, just above a list of Izzy's vital details. The paper bore the same embossed state logo I'd noticed on all Izzy's paperwork.

"Thanks," I said. "I'm just being cautious."

"I understand," he said. "Shana told me a little about why you're here. Is Isabella around, so I can check in with her?"

It only made sense that the state needed to have eyes on the foster children in its care, so I opened the front door and called into the kitchen, "Izzy! Could you come out here a minute?"

Izzy hurried onto the porch, giving Colin a cautious wave before sitting on the rocker next to me.

"Good to see you, Isabella. I'm Colin, your new case worker. I'm glad to see you're doing well here." He turned back to me. "It sounds like the farm is adequately stocked, but I'm a little concerned about you two being so out of reach. Tell you what—I'll drop by next week too, just to verify that vehicles can get in and out of the driveway in case of emergencies."

"Actually, we won't be here that long," I hurried to explain. "Once we can travel, we'll be moving to another shelter until I'm able to find a place to rent. I'll be staying in touch with Shana about that, since we've already discussed it."

He leaned back in his rocking chair, balancing his clipboard on his lap. "Ah, Shana must've told you about the data leak on Isabella. I totally understand your concern. Our office will support you any way we can, so consider us a resource, as well."

"Thanks." I peered into the door screen, and it looked like Jude was no longer standing outside his room. Lowering my voice, I said, "As a matter of fact, I wondered if you could take that man you saw inside—Jude—into town for a visit to urgent care. He's sprained his ankle quite badly. But I'm not quite comfortable with him being here, since he kind of showed up out of the blue."

Colin lowered his brow, concern wreathing his features. "I understand. I'll be happy to take him in. I could probably get him into a hotel or bed and breakfast for the time being. There's no reason for him to stick around."

"I agree. We don't have any fresh ice for his swollen ankle, anyway."

Izzy gave me a worried look. I wasn't sure what

she was thinking, but I knew I had to act in her best interests and get the injured stranger out of here.

Colin stood. "I'll go find Mrs. Cooper and let her know I'll be taking Jude into town. It seems like you're well set for now, but I'll plan to come back early next week, if you haven't moved out by then. If anything changes, please notify Shana and me." Pulling a pen from his pocket, he scrawled a number on one of his business cards and handed it to me. "Just call or text at this number."

"Will do," I said.

As he headed into the house, I turned to Izzy. "I know you like Jude, but we can't let that cloud our judgment. He has that news article about you. The farther away he is, the better. It'll buy us a little more time on the farm."

She finally managed a grateful grin. For the first time in a long time, I started to breathe a little easier.

SIX

Jude surprised me with his eagerness to ride in with Colin to see someone in urgent care. His ankle must've been hurting far worse than he'd let on. As Izzy played with Darius in the TV room, I helped Jude lurch down the front porch steps and ease into Colin's SUV. Maggie carried Jude's backpack to the vehicle and handed it to him.

"Thanks for all your help, ladies," he said, stuffing the backpack onto the floor by his feet. "Colin knows a good hotel in town that'll have generators, so I should be comfortable there. Maggie, I appreciate your hospitality, and the use of the crutches."

Colin leaned toward us from the driver's seat. "I'll bring those back the next time I visit."

"Thank you," Maggie said. "It was nice meeting both of you." She patted the car door, then slowly turned and headed for the porch.

"Thanks for checking on me in the woods and

bringing me in," Jude told me. "I shudder to think what would've happened if you hadn't heard me."

I shuddered to think what might've happened if he'd stayed at Cooper's Corner, so close to my daughter, but I forced a smile. "It was the least I could do. I hope your ankle heals up fast." I gave the men a wave. "See you later, Colin."

I headed for the porch, standing next to Maggie until the SUV was out of sight.

She turned to me, her face serious. "Colin hinted you were worried about Jude and wanted him out of the house. Were there some red flags I missed?"

"He had a news article on Izzy on his nightstand, from when she was small," I said. "I think he was tracking her down for some reason."

She let out a whoosh of breath. "You're thinking he might be her stalker."

I frowned, thinking of Jude's clear-eyed gaze as he said goodbye. He didn't seem the least bit distressed to be leaving the farm.

"I'm not sure," I said slowly. "I can't understand why he'd be stalking her in the first place. If he has some kind of perverse obsession, it seems like the police would've had him listed as an offender in our area. But I don't recall his photo in the ones they showed Izzy."

"Do you want me to call our police station and let them know he's heading into town?" Maggie offered. "I know an officer who'd be glad to look into his records."

"Did he even share his last name?" I asked.

She thought for a moment, then shook her head. "I don't think so."

"And his first name might be assumed," I went on. "As long as Izzy and I stay here, I think we'll be fine. Didn't Jude say he'd parked way up over the mountains and hiked in? So he doesn't even have a vehicle to return to Cooper's Corner if he wanted to."

"He told me he planned to go home as soon as his ankle had healed enough to walk," she offered. "I think he said he was from the Fairlea area."

Fairlea was within driving distance of Izzy's school. An hour-long drive, but still too close for comfort.

That gave me all the more reason for me to look for a place in the northern part of the state where we could hide. Jude knew our location now. Even though he might take some time to return, I had to assume he would, if he was Izzy's stalker.

Maggie seemed to be thinking along the same lines. "We'll do whatever it takes to help you two out," she said.

"Thank you. I think we'll be okay tonight, since he'll be busy getting checked out, then settled into a hotel. I know you could use our help while the power's out. Izzy and I can tote water for the animals or do whatever chores you might have."

Maggie looked thoughtful. "I know you're allergic to bees, but what about Izzy? I could really use some help with my hives, since I need to introduce a new queen tomorrow. The drones attacked the old queen and killed her, probably because she wasn't laying eggs. My friend down the road had a healthy queen with no hive, so he dropped her off a few days ago, and I've been letting the bees get acclimated to her while she's in a queen cage. Thankfully, they've been feeding her, so that's a good sign they've accepted her pheromones. But I really need to release her soon."

"You have beekeeping gear she could wear?" I asked. It sounded like a tricky operation, and I wasn't sure if it was something Izzy would feel comfortable with. Still, I knew she wasn't allergic to bees, since it wasn't in her records, and she'd shared about how she'd run into a hornet's nest at one of her early foster homes. They had smeared toothpaste on the stings and hadn't given her a drop of antihistamine, but she'd managed to head back out into the yard to play the exact same night.

"Oh, yes, I have two suits," Maggie said. "She'll just have to keep the smoke going so I can safely release the queen. The bees aren't going to come at her while she's holding that smoke. They'll be scurrying to care for the new queen, so that'll make them pretty subdued."

"I'll ask Izzy about it," I said. "If not, is there anyone else who could help?"

"Walt knows how, but he's so busy with the cows and cleaning up the property. Angel's deathly afraid of bees, and Kenya said she'd rather not mess with them, either. But I'm not worried about it. If worse comes to worst, I'll try and handle it myself."

I admired her independent spirit, but I hated for

her to do that. "I'll ask Izzy," I said. She was old enough to decide if she could handle a beekeeping chore, and it sounded like she'd be at minimal risk of getting stung. She could always take my Epipen along, just in case.

I could almost feel the late-afternoon sun peeling the paint from the weathered porch floor. "Let's get inside," I suggested. "It's too hot here in the direct sun. Izzy's going to make omelets for our supper, so she'll be happy to throw in any veggies you want to use up. I'll plan to help Rae with the cows so Walt can take a breather." I didn't mention that Walt had seemed overly winded after his extended fence repair. It wasn't good for him to wear himself out when he'd be needed in plenty of other ways in the days ahead.

Maggie thanked me before leading us back into the shade of the house. "I hate that things aren't even cooling down at night," she said. "There's no relief without air conditioning or fans."

"Do you have any generators?" I asked.

"Unfortunately, we don't. We never got around to buying one after that last storm. There are always more pressing needs."

Money must be tight when running a working farm that doubled as a shelter. "Do you all get any outside funding?"

"A small amount. Cooper's Corner falls under the umbrella of the family resource center in town, but they have limited funds. We wind up covering a lot out of our own pockets, since we want to leave plenty for the family programs they're running. The farm generates some income of its own, thanks to the eggs, honey, and beef we sell during the year."

I was starting to understand why it was imperative that Maggie get the new queen bee settled into her hive as soon as possible. "I'll help Izzy with the omelets and ask her about working with the bees tomorrow," I said.

Maggie gave me a grateful look. "You certainly have a heart of gold, Twila. It's beautiful how connected you are with Izzy. She's such a sweetie, and so good with little Darius. He's going to miss her when you leave."

We would miss it here, too. But it wasn't worth the risk of staying, if Jude decided to come back. Tonight, I'd use whatever battery power was left on my phone to search for another shelter we could move to.

IZZY'S OMELETS were as tasty as I'd guessed they would be, and everyone raved over them. From the spinach, mushroom, and feta version to the ham, pepper, and Swiss one, everyone found one they enjoyed.

Rae sighed, wiping her mouth with a napkin. "Delicious, Izzy." She turned to Walt. "Are you ready to head out?"

I stepped in. "Actually, I planned to work with

you tonight, so we can give Walt a little break. We're just hauling water to the cows, right?"

Walt shot me an appreciative look. "That's right nice of you, Miss Twila. But that's a heavy load."

Rae quickly got on board with my plan. "We'll make several trips to the creek. We can load smaller buckets onto the skid steer, then we'll dump them into the watering trough together."

Walt nodded his approval. "You're turning into a regular farm hand, Rae. I don't know what I'll do when you have to move on."

She gave him a pleased grin. "Maybe I won't be so easy to get rid of."

I glanced at Izzy, catching the wistful look on her face. She liked the farm, more than she could express. She'd been eager to help Maggie with the bees, instantly agreeing to suit up and run the smoke for her tomorrow. I was proud of her initiative.

Rae stood, stacking my dirty paper plate on hers. "We'd best head out before it starts getting dark. You ready?"

"I didn't bring boots," I said. "Is there an extra pair around?"

Maggie nodded. "We have quite a few sizes in that bin outside the kitchen door. Take whatever fits."

"I'll see you soon," I said to Izzy. "Just stay inside, please." She nodded, then turned toward Darius, who was urgently tapping her arm with his spoon.

Kenya rolled her eyes, giving him an exasperated smile. "You've got ants in your pants, son."

As Rae dumped the trash, I tried on boots until I

found a pair that fit reasonably well. Together, we stepped onto the side porch. I'd hoped for a breeze, but the air was still uncomfortably warm.

"Izzy seems to be enjoying herself here," Rae observed.

I slowed to stare at the hot pink and orange ribbons fanning out behind the rolling mountains. "It really is beautiful," I said. "We don't see much of the sunset from our apartment."

Rae led the way to the barn. "You might get attached to this place. I feel like I have. It's peaceful."

I helped her load empty buckets onto the skid steer. "I wish we could stay, but that's not possible." After a moment's hesitation, I explained that I'd found an old news article on Izzy in Jude's room.

She raised her dark eyebrows. "No kidding. That's strange. Did you ask him why he had it?"

"The direct approach didn't seem best in that scenario," I said. "I was just glad I found out in time and managed to get him shuttled out of here. At least he's in town now, but I don't want to make it easy for him to find Izzy a second time."

She climbed into the driver's seat of the skid steer. "So you were the one to set that up with Colin? Nice job, mama bear."

As she turned on the engine, I noticed movement toward the far end of the driveway. I was able to make out a shadowy figure walking—or rather, limping—his way through the front woods. My stomach dropped as his massive build and thick beard came into view, removing all doubt as to who it might be. I pointed Jude out to Rae.

She squinted. "Well, speak of the devil," she said. "What happened to his crutches?"

"He doesn't seem to have them," I said grimly. Why would Jude be staggering his way back to Cooper's Corner as night was falling?

And how did he even get here in the first place?

SEVEN

Rae glanced up at the dusky sky. "We need to get rolling while we can still see. It might take a few trips to fill the trough. We don't have time to play catch-up with Jude."

I glanced at the shadowy figure approaching the farmhouse. "I understand, but let me run in and tell Izzy to stay in her room until I'm back."

Rae nodded and pulled the skid steer forward, effectively blocking me from view as I jogged toward the house. Once inside, I spoke to Izzy, who was sitting on the couch, then I told Walt and Maggie that Jude was making his way up the drive. Maggie shot me a significant look, as if she understood my worries and would be on guard.

By the time I headed out of the picket fence gate, Rae had pulled toward the side woods and Jude was within shouting distance. I couldn't very well dash off without checking in with him, otherwise he might be tipped off as to my suspicions.

I gave him a halfhearted wave and shouted, "Back so soon? Did you get a ride?"

He yelled back, "Colin dropped me off. My ankle's not broken—just a bad sprain. I'm supposed to be using my ankle to get the swelling down more. I picked up a compression wrap at the drugstore, but by the time I got to the hotel, it was already booked with locals who need the air conditioning."

Rae made a desperate motion for me to hurry up, then kicked the machine into gear. "Nice," I said. "We have to water the cows now, so I'll probably talk to you later." Even though I didn't really want to.

I raced off to follow the skid steer into the woods, where Rae had come to a stop near the creek. After hurriedly filling seven five-gallon buckets and loading them, we headed toward the field to fill the trough. Curious cows ambled closer, leaving us little room to maneuver the buckets, but we managed not to spill too much water.

Rae glanced at the trough. "One more trip to the creek ought to do it," she said. "I'll head that way."

She took off in the skid steer and I followed behind, noting how badly the machine bounced along the rutted dirt path into the woods. It couldn't be an easy ride, but to her credit, Rae never complained.

Once we'd finally tipped the final bucket into the trough, Rae took another look. The water didn't reach the top, but it wasn't far from it.

"That should be enough for tonight, given what was left in there. But we'll have to refill it in the morning." Rae sounded weary. "I hope the power comes on soon to get the water flowing. I'm worried Walt will have a heart attack with all this lifting."

I hadn't enjoyed all the strenuous manual labor either, but I didn't want to see Walt overburdened. "I'll help you in the morning," I said. "Then maybe Kenya could pitch in again."

Rae nodded as she loaded the empty buckets. "Thanks, Twila. You've been really helpful." She slid into the seat and flipped on the lights. "It's getting dark fast. Why don't you head back inside, and I'll close the gates and park the skid steer. I can see what I'm doing, but you won't be able to for long."

Since the skid steer only had a single seat, I'd need to walk home. I gave her a thumbs-up, then took off down the mowed path toward the house. Lightning bugs drifted up in front of me, and I fought the childish urge to catch one.

By the time I reached the picket fence, I could no longer hear the steady hum of the skid steer. But Rae was familiar with her route, and she had lights to aid her in getting back to the barn.

I chucked my boots into the bin and went in the kitchen door. After washing my hands, I joined Kenya, who was reading a story to Darius by candle-light in the living room. Jude was nowhere in sight, and his bedroom door was closed. I assumed Izzy had followed my instructions and locked herself in our room.

Toting a battery-powered candle, Walt made his way downstairs. He gave me a polite nod. "This darkness makes a body want to get to bed early, doesn't it? Maggie's already asleep. Did everything go okay with the water?"

"It did. Rae's on her way back now," I said. "I'll help her again in the morning."

"Well, I'd appreciate that. It'll free me up to take feed to the goats."

"We fed the cats tonight," Kenya offered, setting Darius down and nudging him toward the stairs. "Izzy's got the magic touch. They won't let Darius anywhere near them."

"Kitty!" Darius' wild screech only served to illustrate why the cats wouldn't get close.

I spoke quietly to Walt as Kenya and Darius headed upstairs. "Jude's staying tonight?"

"Maggie would've turned him away, but Jude said the hotels are full. I plan to take him into town in the morning, and I'll talk with our friend who runs a bed and breakfast. She should be able to make up a small room for him, so he can stay there until he's able to drive again."

For the first time, I considered the fact that Jude had sprained his *right* ankle, which would make it difficult to press the gas or brake.

"That's okay—I understand." I grabbed a couple of solar lights from the table. I didn't want to linger downstairs, in case Jude emerged from his room for a snack. "I'll see you in the morning," I said, heading up.

HALF AN HOUR LATER, a rough knock sounded on our bedroom door. I hesitantly opened it a crack, only to see Walt standing outside, holding a flashlight.

"I need your help." He shifted on his feet. "Rae never did come back. I checked on the chickens because I thought I heard a fox bark, but I didn't see any around. On my way back, I noticed the barn door was still open. I went to close it, but saw the skid steer wasn't parked inside. I went out looking, and found it parked just outside the pasture gate."

"What? That's where I last saw her," I said.

He gave a grim nod. "That's what I figured, so I woke Angel. She checked Rae's room, and she's not in there. Angel's waiting in the front yard with a flashlight, if you think you could join us. I didn't want to wake up Kenya and the child, and it wouldn't make sense to wake Maggie, either. She can't see well in the dark, so she wouldn't be of much help."

I hated to leave Izzy behind, but there was no other option. Rae should've returned a long time ago.

Izzy gave me an encouraging nod from the bed, so I knew she'd heard the entire conversation. I locked the door behind me and followed Walt downstairs. Once I'd pulled my boots on, we met Angel in the front yard. She was gripping a small flashlight, and she silently locked arms with me as Walt led the way toward the pasture. None of us spoke a word, but our concern seemed to charge the very air around us.

We reached the pasture gate, slowing as we

approached the abandoned skid steer. Why hadn't Rae driven it straight to the barn, as she'd planned to do?

Walt played his flashlight beam over the machine's yellow frame. "I checked it out earlier and saw nothing out of place." He turned his flashlight toward the watering trough.

The cows shifted as we made our way through the darkness. Only a sliver of moon hung in the sky. I couldn't shake the feeling we were being watched—if only by cows.

Walt strode directly to the trough and shone his flashlight into the water, as if searching for Rae in its murky depths. I prayed he wouldn't find anything. Angel squeezed even closer while angling her light to help him.

"Nothing," Walt said. He moved his beam in a slow circle around the field, lighting the cows' eyes with an eerie glow. Some were standing closer than I'd thought, and I could even hear them chewing their cud.

Angel turned, training her dimming light toward the ground, as if Rae's body might be lying somewhere beneath the herd.

"Do you have bulls?" I asked. Maybe one had attacked Rae.

"Not right now," Walt said.

Angel spoke in a near-whisper. "What if he found her? Her abusive ex, I mean? Or one of her dealers? They tracked her down the last time she checked into rehab."

I tried to maintain a level head. "It would be incredibly difficult for anyone to track Rae here, much less find her in the dark pasture. I would've seen someone coming up the driveway, if that were the case." I hesitated. "Someone other than Jude, I mean."

But Jude's arrival *did* coincide with Rae's disappearance. Had he gone directly into the house, like I'd assumed? Sure, at some point he'd gotten Maggie's approval to stay overnight, but maybe he hadn't gone directly to his room afterward. Since Maggie was still asleep, I couldn't ask her.

Jude could be outside right now.

Maybe Rae had run into him and started asking uncomfortable questions about the article on Izzy. Maybe he'd snapped and attacked her.

Walt tapped at his blinking flashlight. "We're not going to find her tonight with these dying batteries. I'll look for her in the morning when I do my chores. You ladies had better get inside and try to get some sleep." He gave a cough. "Not to sound harsh, but Rae was here because she was trying to kick drugs. Maybe she fell back into them. Wouldn't be the first time that's happened."

Angel groaned, but didn't deny it was a possibility.

As we filed back to the farmhouse, I tried to make sense of Rae's sudden disappearance. A relapse didn't fit with her eagerness to reunite with her daughter and her determination to look out for Izzy. But the little contact I'd had with addiction had shown me that no one was immune to its power.

The house was completely dark as we shed our boots and crept into the kitchen. I glanced at the space below Jude's door as I walked past for glimmers of light, but saw none. Perhaps he was actually asleep.

Was I giving too much weight to the news article, working myself up over nothing? It seemed unlikely. It was sitting right on Jude's nightstand, and given its crumpled, yellowed state, he might've held onto it for years. On top of that, he'd brought it along on his hike, which happened to run along the property where we were staying. That couldn't be a coincidence.

I let myself into our room, then locked the door behind me. Izzy was still awake, trying to read by the light of a color-shifting solar flower. The room was uncomfortably hot. Even though all the windows were open, the stagnant, muggy air was oppressive.

Izzy looked up at me, a question in her eyes.

"We didn't find her," I said. "We couldn't tell what happened. Walt suggested she might've slipped back into using drugs, but I'm not so sure."

Izzy frowned and shook her head, as if that couldn't be the solution.

"I agree. It doesn't seem like her. She was just telling me how much she loves farm life." I headed into the bathroom to wash up and get into my pajamas, then joined Izzy on the bed. I patted her hand. "We'd best get some sleep. Much as I'd like to stick around, I think we'll try to leave tomorrow, soon as I've watered the cows and you've helped Maggie with the bees."

Izzy shrugged, as if this wasn't the first bitter disappointment of her young life. And it certainly wasn't. I hated to be the one who had to wrench her from yet another positive environment, as we'd had to do with her school.

Anger surged through me at the injustice of it all. Izzy had done nothing wrong, yet she was being tormented by some faceless predator. At least she was with me, as opposed to her previous foster parents, who'd been indifferent about what was going on in her life. It was possible she'd been stalked when she was with them, but no one had noticed.

But now she was with me. And I was the brick wall they'd have to throttle themselves against before harming one hair on Izzy's innocent head.

EIGHT

I woke up sweaty, with my covers kicked off. The night air hadn't cooled things off one bit. I closed our windows and curtains against what promised to be a scorcher of a day. Once I'd helped water the cows, I'd try to set up a reservation somewhere—if I could get decent phone service. A hotel would suffice until I could find a more permanent place to stay.

I headed down to the kitchen, but no one was in sight. Glancing out the window, I saw Kenya cooking on the grill outside and Darius playing contentedly with plastic trucks in a sandbox. I grabbed my shoes and went out to join them.

"'Morning," Kenya said cheerily. "It's a hot one, isn't it?"

I nodded. "I'm happy to help with the cooking before I head out."

Darius made some beeping noises before crashing one truck into another.

"You dumped your load," I said. "Better back it up."

He gave me a serious look and got to work scooping up the sand.

Kenya gestured toward a plate. "Would you mind?"

I brought it over, and she placed the cooked bacon on it.

"He's gotta keep busy, that one. I know it'll be a blessing someday," she continued. Her smile fell. "Maggie told me Rae's gone missing. Walt's already out looking in the back woods for her. I offered to help, but he said it was a one-man job."

I covered the plate with tinfoil. "Izzy and I will likely be moving out later today, but I'll look around too, after watering the cows."

"Now, I really hate to hear that." Kenya pointed toward her son. "Darius told me last night he plans to marry Izzy. You really want to break up a romance that strong?"

I chuckled. "Tell you what. I'll give you my email, and he can send her messages that way. It would mean a lot to her. Plus, I'd like to stay in touch with you."

"It's a deal, then." Kenya systematically flipped several eggs, then shook salt and pepper over them.

One by one, people trickled into the dining room for breakfast, with Jude pulling up the rear. He wasn't using crutches, although he still wore the compression wrap around his ankle. His khaki shorts revealed a tattooed thigh, but I didn't want to stare to find out what kinds of designs he'd chosen.

"You're walking better today," Angel noted.

He sank into a chair. "I think I overdid it yesterday, walking up that drive. It's a lot longer than it looks at first glance."

"Why didn't you have Colin drive you up to the back porch?" Maggie asked.

"The doctor was adamant that I hadn't been walking enough. Colin suggested I could walk the drive, and at the time, I thought it was a good idea." He gave a rueful smile. "I guess I learned otherwise."

Kenya glanced around. "Where's Walt?"

"Still looking for Rae, I'd imagine," Maggie said. "But it's already blazing out there. Let's go ahead and eat without him. I know he'd want us to get moving on our chores."

The bacon and eggs were good, but I couldn't really savor them since I was worrying about who would help me move the water. Had Kenya or Angel driven the skid steer before? Someone would have to stay behind with Darius, since Izzy and Maggie would be out as well. Maybe Walt would show up soon, but I couldn't count on that. He was determined to find Rae, and she was more important than any chores.

I leaned in toward Angel and asked if she could help, but she said she'd nearly wrecked the four-wheeler the other day. "I don't have a lot of driving experience," she said. "Let's just say my ex didn't like me leaving the house." Her lips tightened.

I felt a pang to know there were husbands in the world who would force their wives to give up their freedoms—even to drive. I wondered if they acted like that from the get-go, or if it was a slow, insidious process of taking control of their wives' lives. Regardless, I was glad Angel had escaped that situation.

As we were cleaning up, I headed into the kitchen and asked Kenya if she knew how to drive the skid steer. "Law, no, honey," she said. "Darius would be about as good at that as I would. I can help you move the water buckets, though."

A deep voice sounded behind me. "Let me help."

I spun to see Jude standing in the kitchen doorway. He was standing with no support.

Struggling to come up with a valid excuse, I blurted, "That's not necessary."

He took a step closer, but didn't reply. Darius, who was playing with plastic spoons, grinned up at him. In one surprisingly swift move, Jude swept the boy up into his arms.

Darius squealed in delight, vainly beating at Jude's shoulders with his spoons.

Kenya smiled at Jude. "He's really taken to you. He doesn't have a lot of good men in his life."

So Kenya had deemed Jude a "good man." And Izzy liked him, too. But I couldn't allow myself to be pulled in by his winsome personality.

"I'll figure it out," I said, a bit too forcefully.

Kenya gave me a questioning look as Jude gently deposited Darius on the floor. Before I could say more, Izzy walked in and gave me a brief hug. She motioned toward the door, letting me know she was getting ready to go to the hives.

"Be careful," I said. "Take my Epipen, just in case. It's in my small white bag."

Izzy gave Kenya and Jude polite nods, then headed back for the Epipen. Jude looked a little perplexed, as if he wasn't sure what she was doing. But he didn't need to know.

If Izzy was his target, it would be best for me to keep him close while she was out on the farm. I decided to completely change course.

"Actually, I could use your help, if you think you could drive the skid steer," I told him. Hauling water would keep him busy while Izzy was out of my sight. She'd be back in the house before we could finish.

He gave me a grateful look. "I've driven farm equipment before, so it won't be an issue. I'll be glad to do something for a change. I feel like I've been mooching off the Coopers' hospitality."

Kenya gave a dismissive wave. "They don't care one bit. They're used to taking care of others, bless their kind hearts."

I headed for the kitchen door and turned to Jude. "I'm ready if you are—I'll just grab my boots and head outside to wait. I'm guessing Walt parked the skid steer back in the barn this morning."

"I'll get ready and join you soon," he said, heading toward his room.

As I walked across the drive, a precocious black

kitten swatted at my legs. I bent to pet it, but it scampered off to its watchful mother.

Maggie stepped out of the barn, covered head to toe in her beekeeping suit. Izzy, too, was suited up behind her, and she carried the metal bee smoker. She gestured to a pocket in her suit, so I knew she'd followed my instructions and brought the Epipen. I blew her a parting kiss, then stepped into the welcome coolness of the barn.

Sure enough, Walt had parked the skid steer in its usual spot. I rolled back the huge barn door to allow Jude to pull out. Hopefully, it wouldn't be hard for him to maneuver the heavy vehicle with his braced foot, but at least he knew *how* to drive it, as opposed to me.

As I placed the empty water buckets in the skid steer, I heard Jude's uneven, heavy footsteps approaching. He walked faster than he had been, but his mismatched boots were throwing him off-kilter. On his injured foot, he'd donned a huge, oversized rubber boot he'd probably dug out of the Coopers' shoe bin. The compression wrap and swelling must've made it impossible to fit his sprained ankle into his own hiking boot.

He held out a bottle of sunscreen as he stepped into the barn. "You need some? It's pretty bright out." He blinked in the darkness, his eyes roving my face. "Although you're tan, so maybe you don't need it as much as I do. I blame it on my German roots."

I had forgotten to put any on. Much as I hated to extend our time together, I could get a light burn in the direct sun, and I couldn't endure *any* kind of burn without air conditioning or fans to cool it.

Taking the bottle, I slathered some on my face, neck, and arms. The pleasant smell of coconut wafted into the air.

"Thanks." The dynamic between us felt relaxed—even comforting—and I struggled against it. I didn't want to be the bug that wound up in the Venus flytrap.

In an attempt to clear my head, I asked, "Will you be able to pull out okay? It's kind of dark in here."

He nodded. "Like I said, I'm no stranger to heavier equipment. You want to meet me at the creek?"

"Sure." I stepped out into a blast of heat as he started the engine. Shimmering waves reflected from the black-topped driveway, so I moved to the grass along the side. I wished I'd thought to pack more tank tops and shorts. Instead, I'd worn rolled-up jeans and a short-sleeved tee, in addition to my socks and tall boots. I hated to abandon my chores to others when we left, but part of me couldn't get away from this extended power outage soon enough.

As I entered the shaded woods, I picked up my pace, reaching the creek about the same time Jude pulled up behind me. He unloaded the buckets, and together, we started to fill them. Once they were full, he picked them up and effortlessly loaded them into the skid steer bucket. I wasn't sure if the strain was good on his ankle, but he didn't seem bothered by the same weight Rae and I had worked together to move.

Rae. I scanned the woods, wondering where on earth she was. Had she made a run for it? Did she relapse? Or had someone harmed her—someone like the man standing in front of me?

I watched Jude's wide back as he loaded the final bucket. An uncontrollable urge to get to the truth swept over me. It was time to demand an explanation, and if he didn't have a good one, I was calling the police. I edged toward the creek, ready to jump it and run, if he decided to come at me.

"I saw the news article on your nightstand. The one that shows Izzy as a child." I kept my tone casual, like I was bringing up the weather.

He whirled around, but didn't move closer. "I wondered if you did."

I tried to read his eyes, but his steady gaze told me nothing. "You'd better tell me what you were doing with that," I said.

He glanced behind him. My muscles tensed. Was he going to grab a bucket and hit me with it? I took another step back.

But he eased into a sitting position on the raised skid steer bucket. "Sorry, I have to take the weight off for a second," he explained. "First of all, let me say that you're a great mom. You have a protective shield around Izzy that everyone can sense. It's impressive."

Where was he going with this? Was he trying to butter me up? I glanced at the ground, but there were no big sticks to use as weapons, should I have to defend myself.

He continued. "Second, it's not *my* news article. I found it in Adam Cooper's nightstand, tucked into an old planner from that year. The year Izzy's mother was killed."

I shook my head, confused. "What do you mean? That there's some kind of connection between the Coopers' son and Izzy?"

He stood and moved to the right of the skid steer. Gesturing toward the upraised bucket, he said, "You're going to need to sit down."

Not on his life. I wasn't coming any closer. My hostile look must've said as much, because he didn't press me to take his abandoned seat. And I wasn't about to sit on the ground, where I'd be at a disadvantage.

He gave a slow blink, then returned to his seat on the skid steer bucket. "Okay. I'm going to tell you everything. I didn't show up here by accident."

I tried to slow my rapid breathing. "I guessed as much."

"I've been looking into Adam Cooper from day one—from the day Izzy's mother Christina Falzone was shot in her apartment. At the time, I was living in the same building as Adam." He took a deep breath. "And Adam was the Falzones' neighbor. He said he and another neighbor heard Izzy crying in the hallway, so she must have walked straight out the open door. He called the police and kept an eye on her until they showed up."

I thought back to what Shana had told me. "Izzy's dad was on a fishing trip, wasn't he? He couldn't get back until the next day or something."

"Right. But, like I said, I lived in that same building. I was working a training assignment nearby."

Suddenly, I was very curious as to what kind of job Jude worked. Especially given the way he said he'd been "looking into" Adam from the start.

"What kind of work do you do?" I asked.

"I was an Army Ranger then. As of last year, I'm retired. But all this time, I've never stopped thinking about what happened to Christina and her daughter. Something didn't feel right about the whole thing. The few times I'd run into Adam in the building, there was something in his eyes. Something calculating and dead. I never believed his story that Izzy just ran out into the hallway."

"You think he took her out there?"

"It's possible. But more importantly, I'm certain he shot Christina."

NINE

I stared. "You're telling me the Coopers' son is a murderer."

His gaze hardened. "It makes a lot of sense, and I'll tell you why. Years later, the police connected Adam Cooper with drug trafficking, but before they could bring him in, he conveniently disappeared."

"How does this tie in with Christina's murder?" I was baffled as to how everything connected, but Jude seemed convinced it did.

"My guess is that Christina caught Adam with drugs. Maybe in the hallway, maybe in his apartment—who knows. He couldn't be sure she wouldn't inform on him to the police, so he shot her. Maybe he didn't realize Izzy was in the house until later, when she showed up in the hallway. By that time, another neighbor was on the scene, so he couldn't very well kill the child."

My head was spinning. "A man has been stalking Izzy lately—are you saying that's Adam?"

He stood up slowly from his seat on the bucket. "I'm sure it is. And he's the one who accessed Izzy's files at the DHHR. I have a friend who's been doing a little cyber tracking for me, keeping tabs on where Adam's been hanging out online. His tip-off about Adam's hacking into the DHHR records led me here."

"Is Adam coming to the farm?" I asked, confused. "Is that why you've wormed your way into the Coopers' home?"

He limped toward me, concern in his eyes. Previously, I would've been on high alert as he drew close, but now I was too worried to care. My gut was telling me that Jude wasn't Izzy's stalker, because his story rang true.

"I'm afraid so. But Twila, there's more I need to—"

A four-wheeler peeled down the driveway, then raced directly into the woods near us. It stopped with a jerk, and Walt stepped off, glaring at Jude with a look that could melt metal.

He extended an arm toward the driveway. "Guess what I found when I was clearing the drive?" His question was clearly directed at Jude.

Jude crossed his arms, but didn't answer.

"I found Colin," Walt went on, his tone icy. "He was in his SUV, which was pulled off the driveway and covered with branches." His arms started shaking. "And he was *dead*. Not from natural causes, either. Killed with some kind of knife." He pointed a shaking finger at Jude. "*You* did it, didn't you?"

When Jude refused to comment, Walt threw me a desperate look. "You need to step away from this man right now, Miss Twila. I don't trust him for a second. I'll take you back to the house." He gestured toward his four-wheeler seat.

That didn't make any sense. Jude had told me he was an Army Ranger, but now Walt was accusing him of being a cold-blooded killer.

I took a couple of steps toward the four-wheeler, but Jude stretched out his arm, effectively blocking me. "You're not going with him," he said firmly. "And I'll tell you why. Colin was his son—Adam. He came here to kill Izzy."

WALT GAVE an unhinged grunt of rage and screamed, "Murderer!" He lunged toward Jude's neck with his hands outstretched, but Jude twisted, deftly grabbing Walt and flipping him to the ground, like some annoying bug.

"Find Izzy!" Jude shouted to me. "Get her out of here!"

He didn't need to tell me twice. I jumped on the four-wheeler, scrambling to understand the controls. I needed to get to Izzy, and the fastest way to her was on this vehicle. I pushed the start button, then squeezed the handle to give it gas. I drove straight forward, then made a sharp turn toward the house. I remembered how to get to the goat pen, so I headed in that direction. Maggie had said the hives were past the goats, toward the treeline.

Unfortunately, I didn't have my Epipen, but Izzy

would probably see my distress and come to me. At least I hoped she would.

I whirred along until I caught sight of two white-suited people standing near a line of boxes. Izzy was standing off to one side, giving the smoker regular squeezes, while Maggie handled a wooden frame covered in bees.

I didn't want to get too close, so I pulled to a stop some distance away.

"Izzy, I need you over here!" I shouted.

She turned, stopping her movements. As the smoke died, Maggie slid the frame back into the hive.

I tried to project my voice. "She has to leave. She has to come with me now."

The screened hat hid Maggie's expression, so I didn't know if she'd heard me. Izzy dutifully set the smoker down on the ground and took a step my way.

Maggie slipped around next to Izzy, wrapping an arm around her shoulders. To my horror, the honey-bees trailed her. One by one, I could see them landing on Izzy's suit, like so many dark specks.

Maggie shook her head. "She can't do that," she shouted back. "I need her here."

I watched as Izzy slid a hand into her pocket, pulling out the Epipen before lurching forward to come to me. But Maggie's arm wrapped around her neck, tightening Izzy's hat so that the mesh pressed against her face. The bees darted closer. It wouldn't take much for them to start stinging Izzy's face.

Maggie shouted, "Stay back, Twila. This isn't your fight. She's not even your child, for goodness' sakes."

That was it. Izzy *was* my child, as far as I was concerned. And she was struggling against Maggie's tightening grip.

I slid off the four-wheeler and raced toward them. As I got close, Izzy managed to extend the Epipen toward me. I made a couple of grabs for it, finally managing to lock my fingers around the tube. After popping off the safety top, I plunged the needle into my thigh. I figured I had about thirty minutes, tops, before it wore off.

Wincing through the pain of the shot, I grabbed Maggie's clenched arm and tried to wrestle it away. For an older woman, she was surprisingly strong, and her vise-like grip tightened against me. I was aware of a strong humming sound, and I felt a sting near my elbow as I battled to free Izzy. I couldn't let go of Maggie's arm to try to scrape the stinger out.

Izzy struck out blindly against the bees and the woman who was trying to strangle her. She'd likely gotten stung, as well.

Nausea and dizziness swept over me, and I wasn't sure if it was a reaction to the sting or to the Epinephrine itself. Ignoring the stinger lodged in my arm, I gathered my strength and charged toward Maggie, ramming into her gut with all my body weight. She finally released her hold and sagged to the ground.

"Go!" I shouted to Izzy.

But instead of running away, she came closer, wrapping an arm around me and pulling me to safety. Maggie continued to writhe on the ground, groaning.

When we reached the four-wheeler, Izzy helped me climb onto the seat, then she sat down in front of me. I frantically brushed at my arm, trying to remove the still-painful stinger.

As Izzy fumbled at the controls, I managed to bark a few rudimentary instructions, but my mind seemed to be slipping. Before Izzy could drive away, Maggie managed to stand, like some video game zombie. She stumbled toward the closest hive, pulling out a bee-covered frame. Holding it in front of her, she moved toward us.

"No," Izzy wailed, tears flooding her eyes. There was no way she could drag me away from the approaching threat in time.

My lips stretched tight, I said, "Run. Find...Jude."

Izzy eased off the four-wheeler, and I prayed she would follow instructions instead of trying anything crazy, like rushing Maggie. Even a non-allergic person could only handle so many honeybee stings. Thankfully, she tore off toward the goat pens, which would give her a chance to survive.

It was more than I would have. Tears flooded my eyes as I realized that might've been the last time I'd see my daughter on earth. But at least I'd die fighting for her.

A rapidly approaching four-wheeler engine roared toward me from the field. Surely Walt hadn't managed to escape Jude? I hunkered down on my seat, trying to make myself small if he tried to attack me.

Maggie was just steps away when Jude zoomed up on the four-wheeler. Using the machine, he blocked her from getting any closer. She staggered, trying to maintain her balance, but fell to the ground. As she shouted at him, bees swirled around her.

Jude dismounted and jogged to my four-wheeler. It only took him a moment to climb on behind me, wrapping a strong arm around my waist. I started to fade out as he drove toward the house, where I vaguely registered the sight of police cars and an ambulance in the driveway. Izzy hurried my way, and just before I crashed, I saw Rae standing right behind her, like some kind of guardian angel.

TEN

I woke up tucked under a light blanket in our shared bedroom, feeling lightheaded. Izzy was sitting next to me, and Rae lounged in a chair in the corner.

Izzy leaned closer, gripping my hand. Her eyes were filled with concern.

"I...I'm feeling okay," I managed.

Rae spoke up, her voice a bit rough. "You must be wondering what happened to me. Jude sent me to get help after he figured out that CPS guy was actually the Coopers' son. He'd always suspected him of murdering Izzy's mom."

As Izzy flinched, Rae said, "I'm so sorry about that, hon. Anyway, Jude recognized Adam, even though he'd grown a beard and dyed his hair darker since Jude had seen him years ago. Adam didn't seem to recognize him, so Jude was able to take him up on that ride to urgent care. He confronted Adam as they headed down the driveway. Adam completely lost it, saying once he'd killed Jude, he'd come back and finish the job he should've finished years ago. He pulled out a gun and tried to shoot Jude, but he didn't get far."

"Jude's a trained Army Ranger," I said quietly. "He came here to protect Izzy."

"It's a good thing he did, too," Rae continued. "Once he'd hidden the truck with Adam's body in it, Jude hurried back to the farmhouse to check on you and Izzy. When he felt sure you were safe, he met me in the field, told me what had happened, and handed me a cell phone. He asked me to walk toward the road, calling the police as soon as I had a signal. He wanted me to get a ride to the police station as soon as I could, to make sure they came out here."

For a man with a severely sprained ankle, Jude surely had gotten around—and just when we'd needed him most.

Rae said, "I made it to the station, but it took *forever* to convince them the Coopers could be involved in anything shifty. Finally, I remembered Jude had told me he'd been a Ranger, so I had them call the Army to verify his identity. Once they did that, they put them through to someone at Army Intelligence who'd served with Jude and knew of his efforts to track down a suspected killer. But the police were also dealing with fallout from the derecho, so it took forever for them to finally roll out here to Cooper's Farm."

"Thank you," I said. "You and Jude saved our lives. Now I realize that Maggie and Walt wanted

Izzy dead every bit as much as their son did. She would always present a threat to Adam, as long as there was a chance she could recall the man who killed her mother. The Coopers must've been biding their time, knowing their son was coming back to tie up loose ends." I thought of how deceitful Maggie had been, pretending to introduce herself to "Colin." She'd been in on his plans, all right...and part of me wondered if she hadn't been the mastermind behind all of them.

"Jude's the one you need to thank." Rae's voice gave an uncharacteristic crack. "That man was devoted to his job of protecting you. He told me he hid behind the dresser by your bedroom door last night, watching for Walt or Maggie to attack. But at that point, they hadn't discovered their son's death, so they had no sense of urgency. Today, when Walt found Adam's body hidden in the truck, he must've walkie-talkied to Maggie to let her know Jude was onto them. She improvised by unleashing the bees on you and Izzy, hoping you'd both get stung to death."

A rap sounded at the door, rattling my senses. "Who could that be?" I asked.

Rae picked up on my fear. "It's not Walt or Maggie—the police took them away. It must be someone else."

"Who is it?" I called out.

"It's Jude." His voice reverberated against the door. "Are you doing okay?"

I gave Rae a nod, and she jumped up to unlock the door. Jude walked in, with very little limping.

"You're doing a lot better," I said. "That's good to see."

"Same with you." He took a few steps closer, looking from me to Izzy. "Thank goodness you're both safe and sound."

I shifted, trying to sit up straighter. "All thanks to you."

Rae stood, giving us a quick smile. "I'd better get downstairs to help Angel with lunch. Now that the Coopers are gone, we're short on help. But we do have some good news—the police said electric crews have been working round-the-clock, and our power will likely be restored today or tomorrow."

Izzy gave a delighted squeal and clap, and I grinned. "I can't wait to crank up the air conditioner. This sting still burns." I turned my arm up to look at the throbbing, hot welt the honeybee had inflicted. If I hadn't gotten enough medication, it would've swollen to five times its size by now. Emergency services must've given me a shot of steroid after I'd passed out.

Izzy discreetly moved to the chair in the corner, allowing Jude to take her place. She had trusted him from the start, and her trust hadn't been misplaced. Even if I wasn't able to adopt her—God forbid—it was comforting to know she had gut instincts that would steer her right in life.

I felt a wave of gratitude toward the man beside me. "Thank you for saving me, and for protecting Izzy from the man who killed her mother."

Jude frowned. "In the truck, I told him I knew his

real identity and what he'd done. I ordered him to drive straight to the police station." He glanced at Izzy, who'd picked up a book, and lowered his voice. "He pulled a gun and told me he'd get rid of me, then he'd go back and kill the girl. He said she wouldn't see it coming. I had to stop him."

"You had a knife with you," I guessed.

"Right. I never travel without it."

"Or without a hidden phone, I suppose. Rae told me you gave her one, along with some money, so she could get in contact with the police."

"I needed someone on the inside who'd be willing to help me, and I guessed that Rae would be the one for the job. She seemed to have bonded with you."

"You chose well. When I told Rae about Izzy's stalker, she offered to watch out for her. She has a daughter, too," I explained.

He gave a nod, as if understanding that Rae's daughter couldn't be here due to difficult circumstances. "Rae did great." He looked over at Izzy. "And she did, too. I hope you don't mind that I explained the situation with Walt, Maggie, and Adam to her. I think it helped put her mind at ease to know her mother's killer has been caught."

"I appreciate that. How can I ever thank you enough for intervening at just the right time? You hiked in just to watch out for my daughter." I fought back a wave of emotion.

He took my hand in his and gave it a gentle squeeze. "It's thanks enough to know Izzy has survived this ordeal. Maybe that sweet child I saw in the apartment building all those years ago can finally start to heal." His eyes brightened. "She thanked me herself, by the way—with her words. It meant the world to me."

So I *hadn't* imagined that Izzy had said "no" back at the beehives. She was finding her voice again.

Jude stood, releasing my hand. "My last name is Hartman, by the way."

"Are you planning to head back home now—and where is home for you?" I wished he would stick around to lend a sense of safety here, but then again, I didn't even know how long I would stay. Would the shelter continue to function without Walt and Maggie at the helm?

"I'm not sure when I'll leave. I've moved around the past year or two, trying to find a good place to settle." He glanced out the window, which offered an excellent view of the surrounding mountains. "I'm finding myself drawn to the Green Bank area—there's something peaceful about feeling disconnected from all the crazy out there, you know?"

Even though my job revolved around handling social media for authors, I knew exactly what he meant. Maybe, with a little thought, I could find a way to blend the best of both worlds—living in a big, green space we could relax in, while still maintaining the client base I'd built.

That reminded me, I needed to get in touch with Alexandra. Her author newsletter was due to come out in a week, and I hadn't been able to line up what we were going to include in it.

Jude seemed to sense my restlessness. "I'll head out and let you rest. I think Angel planned to bring up lunch for you two."

"I hope you'll stay here awhile," I said. "I'm sure Rae could use some help with the cows. I'm not much good at it."

His eyes searched mine, and I felt a blush creeping up my cheeks. "Sure, I'd be glad to help until they figure out what's going to happen to this place," he said finally.

As he strode out of the room, Izzy's face snapped up and she gave me a smug grin. She pointed at the door, then made a heart symbol with her hands.

My girl didn't miss a thing.

ELEVEN

Four Months Later

Izzy stood next to me, wearing a pink floral dress and her Doc Martens. She had two tight French braids running along the sides of her head, and her cheeks were rosy. Today was a special occasion—the day the family resource center officially renamed Cooper's Corner after its most notable benefactor, renowned author Alexandra Dubois.

Alex herself was standing on my other side, looking very authorish with her huge sunglasses, black tee, and black jeans. She had been quick to donate an exorbitant amount, once I'd explained that the women's shelter needed help staying afloat. She shared that her ex-husband had been emotionally abusive, and she wanted other women to know the peace she had longed for during her married years with him.

Now she was remarried to the enigmatic, curly-haired man at her side. Henry was the strong, silent type, but watching how he supported Alex throughout the ribbon-cutting event gave me hope that late-in-life romances did sometimes work out incredibly well. He couldn't take his eyes off her the entire time, and once she'd given a very brief, but somewhat awkward speech about the importance of the shelter, he wrapped a long arm around her and wordlessly pulled her into a tight hug.

Rae walked over once the speech was over and the crowd had started to disperse. "We're so honored you came," she said to Alex. "Twila and I are looking forward to running the Dubois Shelter for many years to come. But we'll have to hire some muscle soon. I'm getting worn out handling all the heavy lifting." She motioned to Jude, who was talking with Izzy and Angel. "Maybe you could recruit that one," she joked.

When Alex gave a halfhearted laugh, I could tell she was exhausted from the day's activities. Her autism made social events especially trying, and she'd been here for a couple of hours. "Thanks so much for coming," I said. "You're welcome to leave whenever you want. Be sure you grab some of Angel's lemonade for the road. If you don't mind, I need to head over and speak to someone."

Alex gave me a grateful nod, and Henry led her toward the house, effectively shielding her from bystanders who'd flocked in just so they could catch a glimpse of the world-famous author.

I made my way over to Jude, who was talking

with Angel. She was planning on sticking around a week longer, then she was moving to Pennsylvania, where her uncle had offered her a job with his company. As I approached, she excused herself to check on her lemonade supply.

"Angel was just telling me that Kenya and Darius are all moved into their new apartment," he said. "That's good to know."

"She sent Izzy an adorable photo of Darius grinning next to a block tower," I said. "She's relieved we're staying here to run the shelter, so other women like her can find a safe haven."

I glanced over at Izzy, who sat crouched next to the black barn kitten. It had grown considerably more tame since we'd been here. I realized that, like me, Jude had positioned himself so he could keep an eye on Izzy, even though she was no longer in danger.

"Thanks for watching out for Izzy." I dropped my voice. "She's safe now, you know."

"I know." He glanced toward the house, which had recently received a fresh coat of white paint. "This shelter can be a haven to all of you now."

He was right. The farmhouse had lost some melancholy aspect I hadn't fully recognized when we'd arrived months ago. The darkness must've stemmed directly from the malevolence Maggie and Walt had harbored toward Izzy—and, by extension, me.

Maggie, in particular, had been determined to shield her family from the consequences of their criminal behavior. When police went through phone texts and messages, they found evidence of their participation in Adam's criminal activities, even going so far as to help him move drugs through their own farmhouse. She and Walt had been involved in their son's drug trade for years.

Walt had crumbled under interrogation, admitting that Izzy's mother had seen Adam drop a bag of heroin in the hallway of their apartment building. When she'd asked him about it, he'd tried to brush her off, but he knew she was going to report him to the authorities. He had quickly taken matters into his own hands, breaking into her apartment that very night and shooting her.

When Maggie was questioned by the police, she'd remained tight-lipped as to her own involvement in the drug racket, although there were plenty of incriminating texts sent from her own phone.

I thought back to the harrowing honeybee showdown. Izzy told me that Maggie had managed to install the queen in her new hive before I'd showed up. Ever since then, Izzy had thrown herself into learning about honeybees—from watching beekeeping videos to talking with the neighbor down the road who'd given Maggie his queen. She had quickly grown comfortable in the beekeeper suit, and looked forward to harvesting honey and selling it.

The roly-poly kitten frolicked across Izzy's hands as I finally asked Jude the question that had been spinning in my mind for weeks. "Since your new cabin is just forty minutes away, I wondered if you might considering helping out with the heavier chores around here. We can't pay much, but we'd really appreciate it, at least until we have more residents." When he didn't answer, I hurried to add, "Good help is hard to find."

"Can we take a walk?" he asked abruptly.

I glanced around. Most of the crowd had already headed home, including the enthusiastic chair of the family resource center who'd headed things up today.

As if to further reassure me, Shana walked over to talk with Izzy, giving me a friendly smile. She'd recently told us that we had an adoption court date scheduled in two months. I was officially going to become Izzy's mom.

With everything well in hand, I told Jude, "Sure. You want to walk toward the woods?"

He nodded, and we made our way up the path.

"I know a lot has happened," he said slowly. "And I appreciate that you trust me to work around here."

"Of course I trust you." I slowed as we stepped into the shaded woods. "You saved our lives."

"I have to be honest with you." His eyes rested on mine. "I've watched how tenacious you are about protecting Izzy, and I know how much you love her. You risked your life to save her out at those hives. You have a warrior spirit and an unbreakable will that demands respect."

His words warmed my heart. "Thank you," I said.

His look intensified. "What I'm inadequately trying to say is that I find you well-nigh irresistible,

Twila. But I don't want to work here if that complicates things, or makes you feel obligated to go out with me."

I couldn't hide the grin spreading across my face. "I'd be more than happy to go out with you. And we'll play things by ear, but for now, we'd appreciate all the help you can give."

He hesitantly stretched out a hand, so I tucked my hand into his. In companionable silence, we headed back toward the farmhouse.

Izzy careened up the path toward us, a striped cat close on her heels. We unlinked hands, but not before Izzy had noticed. Her eyes shone as she approached.

"Jude's going to help out on the farm," I said. "Maybe he could teach you some survival skills while you're homeschooling."

Her lips quirked into a pleased smile. She hurried over to walk alongside me, linking her arm under mine. As we neared the farmhouse, Jude hurried over to help Rae and Angel take down a folding table in the front yard.

Izzy stopped short and turned, her blue eyes seeking mine.

"I love you, Mom," she said. Her words—the words she'd finally found—came out strong and confident. I pulled her into a close hug, patting her back as if she were my baby.

"I love you, too," I murmured. "You'll always be safe with me."

ABOUT THE AUTHOR

HEATHER DAY GILBERT, an RWA Daphne du Maurier Award-winning author and 2-time ECPA Christy Award finalist, enjoys writing contemporary mysteries with unpredictable twists, much like the Agatha Christie books she read growing up. Her novels feature small towns, family relationships, and women who aren't afraid to protect those they love.

Sign up for Heather's newsletter at **https://heatherdaygilbert.com/** to receive a FREE ebook download of HOUSE BLEND, a standalone novella in the bestselling, 9-book *Barks & Beans Cafe* cozy mystery series.

And if you'd like to know more about fictional bestselling author Alexandra Dubois, referenced in *Queen Bee,* be sure to check out Heather's clean, twisty psychological thriller *Queen of Hearts*.

www.ingramcontent.com/pod-product-compliance
Lightning Source LLC
LaVergne TN
LVHW090615110826
845146LV00001B/396

* 9 7 9 8 9 8 7 5 5 6 9 8 6 *